MW01488046

Return Trip Ticket

DAVID C. HALL

ST. MARTIN'S PRESS
NEW YORK

Design by JUDY CHRISTENSEN

Production Editor: SUZANNE MAGIDA
Production Manager: MARNI SISKIND

Library of Congress Cataloging-in-Publication Data
Hall, David.
      Return trip ticket / David Hall : introduction by David Westlake.
          p. cm.
      "A Thomas Dunne Book"
      ISBN 0-312-08283-5
      I. Title.
    PS3558.A365R48   1992
    813'.54—dc20   92-27466
                                                   CIP

First Edition: December 1992

10 9 8 7 6 5 4 3 2 1

ACKNOWLEDGMENTS

The author and the publisher wish to thank Donald E. Westlake for allowing us to use his introduction, written for the Spanish edition of *Return Trip Ticket* and subsequently reprinted in *The Armchair Detective*, in this edition of the book. We also thank *The Armchair Detective* for their cooperation in providing us with it.

INTRODUCTION
Donald E. Westlake

THE TARNISHED KNIGHT

The private eye entered fiction over sixty years ago, with Dashiell Hammett and the other writers of *Black Mask,* a pulp magazine published in New York. Fifteen years later, Raymond Chandler would define the private eye as that tarnished knight going down the mean streets, but at first he was merely a fallible human being, with some toughness and self-respect, trying to do his job against stiff opposition.

That job, the private eye's job, was to be what is nowadays called a rent-a-cop, a fairly seedy and shabby occupation at best. He wouldn't be a private eye if he were qualified for anything loftier, but the point was then, and the point is now, that his lack of qualification is only in education and necessary establishment contacts; in terms of pride and courage and determination, his qualifications are among the best.

So the private eye's job is shabby, but his *purpose* is to keep his dignity by doing the shabby job with nobility. That's the tension that created the private eye in the first place, and keeps him still alive these many years later, though only when he's in the hands of a writer who understands the tension, who knows that the private eye is as much *tarnished* as *knight*.

The world has changed over the decades, God knows, but the private eye's relationship to the world has remained more or less constant. "Emotions are nuisances in business hours," Hammett's Continental Op once said, and today's private eye still tries to keep a surgeon's dispassion toward the people who cross his professional path. As more history has encrusted on his broad shoulders, though, dispassion has become a rare coin. These days, it's hardly more than the surface he tries to keep cool, disguising whatever heat rages within. It was only when he was very young—as young as the century—that the private eye could at will turn the emotional flame down all the way.

"It was a wandering daughter job," began "Fly Paper," a 1925 Continental Op story in *Black Mask*, defining forever one of the principal components of the private eye's ongoing opera. It is rich people who have both the money to afford a private eye and the complexity of life to need his services. Rich people have children who, because they grow up rich (because they grow up, in fact, with precisely the "qualifications" the private eye lacks), believe lazily that they can understand the world without having to study it. This belief leads them to underestimate companions who wish to use or abuse them. The child's entanglement with unsavory companions leads the parent to call in the tarnished knight, the only man who combines sufficient knowingness (enough to be able to conquer the unsavory companions) with sufficient nobility not to become an unsavory companion himself. When the child is a daughter, a grown daughter, a wandering daughter, the story reaches even more deeply into the realm of timeless myth, the story of the knight and the damsel, tarnished knight and tarnished damsel, worldly man and *faux* worldly woman.

David C. Hall's *Return Trip Ticket* honorably continues and extends this story, remaining true to its finest antecedents while stretching its range to include the reality of today, those facts of our world which didn't exist sixty years ago, when the predecessors of Hall's private eye, Wilson, were born. It would be unfair to Hall's story to point to the specific points of contemporary reality he uses—they emerge in their proper place in the unfolding of the

viii

plot—but at least it can be pointed out that Wilson's world is *broader* than the Continental Op's. Personville, upstate, was about as far as the Op ever traveled, and a telegram from New York or Baltimore was about as far as his knowledge extended. Wilson's world is *the* world; it is as necesssary for him to learn Barcelona as Chicago or the desert of the American Southwest.

Wilson is also more cynically knowing and negative about himself than are his earliest predecessors. The Op and his contemporaries, wrapped in their professionalism, were reasonably content about themselves. Very early on in *Return Trip Ticket*, we get this from Wilson:

There was nothing to think about, it was just a matter of keeping on, and there was nowhere to go but straight. Eventually she would get tired. Everybody gets tired, everybody makes mistakes. Which was why, Wilson thought, you didn't have to be very smart to do his job.

This world-weariness is simply one more antagonist for the private eye to fight, possibly to conquer. Wilson's professionalism has less pride to bolster it, and so it must bolster itself. He's a pro merely because he's a pro, not because he finds much by way of nobility in his calling, nor in his associates. His relationship with his boss at the detective agency is touching in its revelation of how the tarnish has spread, how the old man-among-men camaraderie has decayed:

[The boss] had been in the detective business for a long time and had accumulated a lot of information, which he wouldn't talk about unless he was drunk. So when he wanted to brief an agent he invited him for drinks. It was a Freudian thing, somebody had said once, like guys who can't have sex unless they're a little loaded.

There's sadness in this book, but there's strength and a kind of victory as well. It is the tradition brought forward into a meaner time, made real again, and finally accepting both the tradition and the new reality. The wandering daughter of *Return Trip Ticket*, in her flight, wanders straight into postmodernism, with all its studiedness and self-awareness and affectlessness, and Wilson, the good detective, follows her all the way.

Return Trip Ticket

1
1988

The first thing Wilson thought of when he saw the gas station, still well off in the distance, was getting the dead bugs cleaned off the windshield. He had been driving a long time, watching them smash one by one on the glass, and he was sick of peering out through the black smudges they had left. Even though there was not that much to look at really, just dry earth and stubbly weeds, the greasy blackness of the hot pavement.

The gas station was a purple sign on a metal stalk, pumps under the shade of a tin roof, a low building with an even coating of motor oil and dust. Wilson pulled in beside the gas pumps and switched off the engine. A skinny kid in dirty jeans and a baseball cap came out the screen door and stood squinting at him with a vague smile. Wilson got out of the car, told the kid to fill it up, and stretched. There were cans of motor oil and some stupid-looking souvenirs on the other side of a dirty window, a yellowed poster for a snake farm four miles down the next side road that had live rattlers. Wilson wondered what kind of people would go four miles out of their way to look at a bunch of rattlesnakes.

"You got anything to drink?"

1

The kid nodded at the red-and-white cooler next to the door. "Got any beer?"

The kid smiled and shook his head. "Can't sell beer at a gas station in this state," he said cheerfully. "There's a tavern in Pearson, about twenty miles down. You gotta turn off the highway, though."

Next to the snake farm probably, Wilson thought, moving stiff-legged toward the cooler. Nothing like looking at rattlesnakes for working up a thirst. He put the correct change in the slot and took a bottle of Coca-Cola out of the cooler and opened it. The carbonation prickled his tongue. There was nothing to see but the gas station, no trees, not even any rocks worth noticing. You could see shimmering veils of light the heat made in the distance, the stuff mirages are made of. He finished the Coke and walked back to the car. The kid was watching the numbers turn over in the little window on the pump.

"Did you see a girl in a yellow Ford come through here this afternoon?"

"What year Ford?" the kid said. His eyes were small and close together, he had grease smears on his nose and a dim, feebleminded-looking smile.

Wilson shrugged. "I don't know. Late model."

"Didn't stop here," the kid said, squeezing out the last gush of gasoline into the tank. "Check the oil and water?"

Wilson nodded, walked back to the cooler and bought another Coca-Cola. When he got back into the car he set the bottle in his crotch. The air-conditioning in the rental car wasn't working very well, and he felt the heat of the vinyl seat through his clothes. When he had paid the kid he started the car and drove out onto the highway. A camper rolled down the other lane like a clumsy plastic egg and then the highway was clear. Wilson pressed the gas pedal slowly to the floor, held it there until the needle hit a hundred, and then let off a little and let it cruise. The hot wind felt good coming through the open window. He opened the glove compartment, took a joint out of a cigarette pack, lit it and turned on the radio.

The sun took a long time going down, and the road ran straight and almost flat between bald sand hills. The mountains were hazy in the distance, far away as stars. There was nothing to think about, it

2

was just a matter of keeping on, and there was nowhere to go but straight. Eventually she would get tired. Everybody gets tired, everybody makes mistakes. Which was why, Wilson thought, you didn't have to be very smart to do his job.

Then there was the darkness around him, only the lights on the highway and the faint glow off the dashboard. Radio stations faded out in the distance, and he twisted the dial looking for new ones. The car seemed like a spaceship, the radio picking up weak signals from the distant earth, traveling across an immense nothingness. A sign loomed up under the lights: RESTRICTED AREA, NO PHOTOGRAPHS. There wouldn't be anything you could see from the highway even in the daylight, Wilson thought, except rocks and dirt and dry weeds, but he wondered what it was they were doing out there that they didn't want you to photograph. He was tired, and stoned by then, and it gave him a weird, science-fiction sort of chill.

They were driving a big, late-model Dodge. The driver winced when he rolled down the window and the hot air hit him in the face. They didn't get out of the car. There were two of them, and they wore light-colored, wrinkle-proof, short-sleeved shirts. Their suit jackets were on hangers in the back. The driver was wearing sunglasses with green lenses and silvery metal rims. The other one had on normal glasses and the tired look around the eyes you get from looking at the glare off the highway.

"You see a girl in an eighty-six Ford come by this afternoon?" the driver said.

The kid took off his baseball cap, ran his hand through his grimy blond hair, and broke into a wide smile. It was about the funniest thing he had heard in a long time, and he rocked on his heels, beaming at the green glasses.

"There was another fella asked me that awhile ago," he said.

"Yeah?" the driver said.

"Fat guy."

The driver nodded. The other one looked at the kid for the first time. He had a round face and a sour twist to his mouth, as if his stomach were bothering him.

"He didn't know what year Ford it was though," the kid said.

"So did you see her?"

3

The kid shook his head. "Didn't stop here. Fill it up?"

The driver nodded. The kid put gas in the car, checked the oil, and put in a little more water.

"I bet this thing really moves out, huh?"

"Sure," the driver said, signing the credit card slip. "When'd this guy come through here?"

The kid looked up, calculating, at the sky. It was almost colorless, just pure light.

"About two hours ago, I guess."

"Uh-huh," the driver said. He took a pack of cigarettes out of his shirt pocket, shook one out, and put it in his mouth. He had big hands with thick blunt fingers, stiff blond hairs growing out of them.

"You guys cops?" the kid said, scratching himself, beaming again.

A faint smile twitched the corners of the driver's mouth under the green sunglasses.

"That's right, kid," he said, starting the engine, "we're the cops."

2

The yellow Ford was parked in the motel lot in front of a door with the number 25 on it. The blue neon sign facing the highway said LAST OASIS MOTEL. A green neon palm tree flashed off and on above the name.

It seemed almost too easy, Wilson thought as he turned off the engine. The radio went on playing, out of some station so far away he could just make out the words: "But, baby, save the last dance for me."

He remembered it, from a long time back, as if his radio had picked up a signal from twenty years before.

The car door made a clunking sound when he closed it behind him. There was no wind and no sound but faint electronic noises drifting out the motel room windows, muffled voices from an unseen television, melodramatic music swelling to a false climax.

Wilson rubbed the back of his neck and grimy sweat slid under his fingers. His eyes felt bloodshot and swollen, bulging out of his head. He walked slowly across the lot with a lumbering, fat man's walk, stopping to glance inside the Ford. There were a couple of empty Coca-Cola cans on the floor, a newspaper on the backseat, empty cigarette packs, nothing very interesting.

He stopped for a moment in front of the door to 25, drew a breath, and knocked. There was no sound from inside. It looked like the sort of door a kid could kick in with his shoes off, but he didn't particularly want to do that.

Then a woman's voice, sounding flat and strained through the door: "Come in."

She was sitting on a double bed with a red plaid spread, barefoot, with her legs drawn up. She was thinner than she looked in the photos he had seen. Her face had lost the baby fat in the cheeks and she looked tired. Her light-brown hair had been cut short and looked as if it hadn't been washed for awhile. There was a six-pack of beer with one can gone on the night table beside her, next to a white paper sack with the remnants of some kind of sandwich on top of it. She was holding an automatic with both hands, her elbows propped on her knees, pointing it at the center of his chest.

Wilson closed the door behind him with his foot and stood there without moving, with his arms loose at his sides. If he had been smart he would have expected something like this, he thought, but he had given up trying to be smart quite a ways back. She held the pistol steady, and that was something. He would have been a lot more worried about it if she had been shaking.

"Are you a cop?"

Wilson shook his head. "No."

"No," she repeated. "If you were there'd be a bunch of them behind you, wouldn't there? Or is there? Is there anybody else out there?"

Wilson shook his head again. She kept the pistol on him, and her eyes. They were a funny shade, he thought, somewhere between green and blue and gray. You couldn't tell in that light.

"Your father hired me to find you," Wilson said.

Her eyes flickered over him lightly, with even a trace of amusement.

"Well, you found me, didn't you?" she said. "What are you going to do now?"

Wilson nodded at the six-pack on the night table. "You think I could have a beer?" He had been thinking about it since he had spotted the six-pack. He was worn out, he had finally found her and that ought to be the end of it, and it didn't seem fair that it wasn't.

6

"You've got a gun, I suppose?"

"Yeah."

She leaned back against the wall, keeping the pistol pointed at his chest. "Take it out with your fingertips and put it on the bed. Slowly. Don't make any sudden movements. If you do, I'll shoot you."

Her voice shook a little then, but only her voice. Her hands didn't move, they didn't even look as if they were getting sweaty.

"I will, you know," she said softly, looking at his eyes for perhaps the first time. Her own eyes were tired, scared maybe, and that, Wilson thought, was to be expected.

"Sure," he said. He tried to sound reassuring, but he wasn't sure it came out that way. There was a big television set in the corner of the room, and he saw her arms, the V of her drawn-up legs and the shape of the automatic, all in blurred reflections on the screen. It reminded him of something, but he couldn't say what.

He reached around behind his back, closed his fingers on the butt of the revolver, and pulled it out of the top of his trousers. He held it out in front of him, dangling from his fingertips like some nasty dead animal, leaned forward, and dropped it on the bed.

She nodded at the brown armchair beside the television set and said, "Sit down."

Wilson let out a soft sigh as he sank into the armchair and almost closed his eyes. She twisted a can of beer out of the pack with her left hand and tossed it into his lap. He opened it and took a long swig.

"How long have you been after me?"

"Since Barcelona," Wilson said. "Your parents hired me to find you."

"So you know . . .?" She didn't finish the question. Maybe she decided the answer was obvious, or maybe she just didn't want to go into it. She took a can of beer for herself, set the automatic on the bed beside her, and watched him as she opened it. He considered telling her she didn't need to bother, but she wouldn't have believed him anyway. She took a drink and leaned back against the wall, stretching out her legs. Pretty feet, Wilson thought. After a moment she took out a cigarette and lit it with a plastic lighter.

"They've been paying you all this time?"

"Sure." It wasn't really all that long, he thought, the way people normally calculate time. It just seemed like it.

"Sure," she said. "They've always been good at paying for things." She took another drink. "What do they want? I mean, what do they want you to do?"

Wilson shrugged. "To begin with they just wanted to know where you were. And then—"

He stopped there. He hadn't thought about it much, maybe he hadn't wanted to think about it. They had both made a big circle, and now he had found her more or less back where they had started from. He should have known her well enough by then.

"I guess you're supposed to take me home to Mommy and Daddy," she said dully, "and they'll get some sharp lawyers—they've probably already got them—and . . ." She shook her head quickly. "I'm not going to do that."

She took a sip of her beer and looked up at him. "So when you finish your beer you can piss off. You can tell them you found me. Tell them I'm fine. Well, as well as can be expected."

Wilson shook the can and felt a little bit of beer sloshing around at the bottom.

"I was thinking about asking you for another one," he said, risking a thin smile. She smiled back, the ghost of a smile that vanished without leaving a trace. He probably didn't look very convincing, a chubby bald man slouched in a plastic armchair with a beer can in his lap.

"What do they know about it?" she said, not looking at him, looking at the wall.

"The agency gave them reports," Wilson said.

"They wouldn't understand it," she said. "They wouldn't understand it if you spelled it out for them."

"You understand it?" Wilson said quietly.

Her eyes snapped to his face, the corners of her mouth tightened.

"I knew what I was doing," she said, a little too emphatically. "As much as anybody does. I'm not going to plead the poor dumb little rich girl. I'm not."

Wilson drank off the rest of the beer and sat there watching her, wondering if she was going to give him another one. The air conditioner made a low continuous hum.

8

"You're not going to get out, are you?" she said after a while. Wilson shook his head and set the empty can on the floor.

"I followed you across the whole fucking country," he said, as if that were some sort of explanation.

"It's real American, isn't it?" she said, looking vaguely at the brown-and-yellow striped motel wallpaper. "You get a car and start driving, keep driving till you get to the end of the world. That's about all that's left of the pioneer spirit."

The end of the world, Wilson thought. Los Angeles maybe. Where it just starts all over again.

She tossed him another beer and opened one for herself. Wilson took a drink and wiped his mouth.

"What are you trying to do?" he said.

"I don't know. Go home, I guess."

3

Any way you figured it she was going in the wrong direction. Her name was Elizabeth Dantry, and she had been born some twenty-six years before, in South Dakota. Her family had not stayed in South Dakota for long. They had an apartment in Chicago now, a house in Seattle, and another one in Colorado. Her father had started out by making a couple of smart deals and then limited himself to not making any stupid ones, on the principle that once you've got money you don't need to take risks to make a lot more of it.

"I suppose you met him, huh?" she said. "So what'd you think?"

"I only talked to him for a few minutes," Wilson said. He knew what he thought about Dantry, but he didn't see any point in going into it. They had finished off the six-pack by then and driven over to the tavern where she had bought it. There was an electric sign behind the bar with sparkling water tumbling continuously over unidentified falls, and the jukebox played sad country-western songs about broken hearts and car payments.

"He's an asshole," she said, with no particular emotion. She slid her glass around in the little puddle of moisture on the bar. "I was crazy about him when I was a kid. He was real good-looking then. I suppose he still is."

Wilson was chewing on a steak sandwich that the bartender had heated up in a little microwave oven without taking the cellophane off. A couple of men in dirty jeans were hunched over the other end of the bar. In one of the booths a woman with fluffy blond hair was drinking a little too fast and talking a little too loud, leaning up against a fat guy in a plaid shirt. She was a big, well-made woman with broad shoulders and deep breasts and a face that needed too many creams and powders to make it look like it used to. The kind of woman who had been raised to live with some cowboy and drive around in pickup trucks, Wilson thought, and there weren't that many cowboys left.

"He was playing croquet one time out on the lawn with this other guy—some big wheel, I don't know—and I came out on the porch. The sun was kind of in my eyes, and the other guy looked sort of like my dad, I guess. Anyway, he scored, and then he jumped up in the air with his mallet in his hand and yelled, 'Yahoo,' and I thought, That guy's an asshole. And then when they were coming up to the house I saw that it was my dad."

Her voice had a flat, droning sound, perhaps a bit wistful. It went pretty well with the music.

"I guess I'd known he was an asshole for a long time. I just hadn't got around to admitting it."

Wilson had flown into Denver, picked up a rental car at the airport, and driven up into the mountains to the house, along a clear, quick-running stream with houses beside it that looked like Swiss chalets or restored goldminers' cabins. The maid left him sitting in an oversize living room with turquoise ashtrays heavy enough to split someone's head and neat stacks of glossy magazines on low wooden tables. There were a couple of colorful Indian blankets on the wall and one enormous buffalo head.

Dantry came in wearing a checked shirt, tight jeans, and slightly scuffed boots. A man in his fifties or perhaps early sixties, he had thick white hair and a deep tan. He carried himself erect, and there wasn't any fat on him that you could see. He gave Wilson a

11

smile and a hearty handshake and said, "Nice of you to come out," as if he didn't know he had paid for the trip.

They sat in big armchairs covered in soft black leather. When Dantry spoke about his daughter the skin around his eyes made fine creases. He looked concerned, as he might have looked concerned talking about his tax problems or the situation in Cambodia. At that time she had just been lost, and maybe rich men were used to their daughters getting lost now and then. They turned up after a while with an undesirable husband, or a competent agency like the one Wilson worked for was hired to go out and find them. Maybe it was just sort of an expensive kind of hide and seek.

"Elizabeth went to Europe in February," Dantry said. "She was going to visit England, France, Italy, travel, just relax for a while, and eventually stop in Spain. She studied comparative literature in college, and she was thinking of doing courses in Spanish lit in Barcelona."

Wilson had taken out a fat pipe and filled it mechanically, pressing down the tobacco with his thumb. Dantry glanced at the pipe once and then made a point of ignoring it. He was probably one of those people who had stopped smoking cold one day, out of sheer willpower and self-esteem. He looked as if he had a lot of both.

"She worked for the *Denver Post* for a while—Sam Mitchell, the editor there, is a friend of mine, of course—but I guess she didn't like the work."

Wilson scribbled in his notebook to make sure there was ink in his ballpoint. "When did you last hear from her?" he said.

"About two months ago. A letter."

"Would you mind my taking a look at it?"

Dantry looked at him with mild surprise in his blue eyes.

"I think my wife's got it," he said coldly, "and she's in Seattle."

Apparently it was not the sort of thing Wilson was supposed to ask for some reason. There were probably others, there usually were.

"Was there anything unusual about it?"

Dantry shook his head. "No. Nothing at all."

"Where was it from?"

"From Barcelona. She was sharing an apartment with a friend

12

from college. When we didn't hear from her for a month we called and the friend said she had moved. They'd had some kind of falling out, I gather, and the girl didn't know where she'd moved to."

"How long ago was that?"

"About two weeks ago."

Wilson wrote that down. "About how often did she usually write you?"

"Every two or three weeks, a month at the most. And we phoned, of course, though that's a little difficult because of the time difference. Elizabeth's not irresponsible. That's why—"

"Did you send her an . . . allowance of some kind?"

"Yes. We'd been sending it to American Express when she was traveling, but when she seemed to have settled for a while in Barcelona I arranged for a bank transfer."

"Do you know . . .?"

"I checked through Fred Willis at Chase Manhattan," Dantry said. "She hasn't made any withdrawals for over a month. That was when I got in touch with your Mr. Haeflinger."

"Uhm-hum," Wilson murmured. Dantry looked more annoyed than worried, so perhaps Elizabeth was not so responsible after all, but that was another question he wouldn't be supposed to ask. "Have you been in touch with the Spanish police?"

"No," Dantry said, wrinkling his forehead. "I thought it would be . . . premature."

"Of course," Wilson said. A guy like Dantry didn't want to have anything to do with any cops. That was why he called Haeflinger. Wilson asked a few more innocuous questions and got innocuous answers. Dantry didn't know of anybody Elizabeth knew in Spain—or the rest of Europe, for that matter—except the girl she had shared the apartment with. Wilson asked for photos and Dantry got a leather-bound album from the bookcase. There was Elizabeth on horseback, Elizabeth on skis, Elizabeth beside the swimming pool, Elizabeth in a long dress at somebody's wedding. It seemed as if during some periods of her life photos had been taken whenever Elizabeth did anything more interesting than getting up in the morning. She looked pretty much like any attractive kid who grew up in the West and whose parents had money: smiling, outdoorsy, a little gawky. A few boys cropped up beside her in the later

13

pictures, broad-shouldered types with clean clothes and clean faces and broad toothy grins, the sort of boys mothers simpered over and fathers slapped on the back. Wilson wondered how many of them had screwed her in the backseat of a car somewhere.

There were a couple of shots of her in Europe, one with a big red backpack beside her, laughing, with the gritty wall of some big station behind her, another one with "Venice, March" written underneath in a neat round hand. She was sitting in a metal chair at some outdoor café, and there was a glimpse of a plaza behind her, with a few pigeons that weren't looking at the camera. She was wearing jeans and a checked shirt, open over an orange T-shirt with something written on it, gazing up at the camera with a kind of reluctant half smile. She looked a little different in that one. She was beginning to look like a woman.

Wilson took three of the most recent photos, telling Dantry he would have copies made and send him back the originals. On the way out he glanced up at the buffalo head again. Close up it looked heavy enough to pull the wall down.

"I shot that one myself," Dantry said.

"Uh-huh," Wilson said. He looked at Dantry and then looked at the buffalo again.

A guy had told him once, in a bar somewhere—in Los Angeles he thought it was—about how they did it. You paid the Fish and Game Department two thousand dollars, and they drove you out onto the buffalo reserve in a pickup truck and found you some buffaloes. Then you got out and walked up to the buffalo you liked, and the buffalo looked at you and maybe sort of wondered—for the buffalo is not a particularly intelligent animal—what the hell you were doing there. Then you lifted a big-bore rifle, the kind of rifle they used to shoot elephants with when shooting elephants was still legal, and shot it, and the buffalo fell down. You got it loaded on the pickup and you got somebody to cut off the head and mount it and somebody else to cut up the carcass, and you put the buffalo steaks in the freezer and served them on special occasions. You had to be an asshole to do something like that, the guy in the bar in Los Angeles had said. A rich asshole, of course.

It was dark when Wilson got back to Denver. He came into the city on a highway lined with drive-ins and used car lots and

14

streaks of colored neon. Kids were cruising the strip in cars with shiny chrome and rumbling engines, with rock 'n' roll blaring out the open windows. Wilson remembered doing that when he was a kid. He remembered that it had felt good but he couldn't remember why.

He pulled into a drive-in, pressed the button under the talk box on the post beside his window, and waited until a voice said, "Take your order please." He ordered a super steakburger, French fries, and a vanilla malted milk. A blonde in a cowboy shirt brought it out to him and gave him a dull smile when he paid for it. He watched her hips shift under her jeans as she walked away, and sucked the malted through a straw. Cars jerked noisily in and out to the music of various radio stations or sat like gobs of colored metal under yellow lights that gave them a sheen of tinselly glamour, and inside the cars kids laughed and threw their arms around or sat intently chewing or sucking on straws while they gazed through the windshields into nothing. Eating his steakburger, Wilson had the abrupt odd feeling that he had fallen into another time zone and that at any moment they might all realize he had no right to be there. A glob of ketchup fell on his seersucker suit. He rubbed it with a flimsy napkin and it left a pale, bloody-looking stain.

He spent the night at a hotel near the airport. The agency had an account with the chain, and all the hotels had the same color scheme, the same music, and the same smell. That was the attraction, of course, that wherever you were you seemed to be in the same place. In the bathroom in his room there was a paper across the toilet seat which certified that nobody had sat on it since it had been disinfected.

Wilson took off his jacket and hung it on the hook on the door, sat down on the bed, and rolled a joint. He smoked it standing at the window, which looked out over a dimly floodlit courtyard with a kidney-shaped swimming pool at the center. The water was a greenish blue under the lights, still, like a sheet of aluminum. He was halfway through the joint when he saw the reddish glow of a cigarette and made out a pair of bare legs crossed in front of a deck chair. He could just barely see them, and for some reason it irritated him that he couldn't see them any better. No doubt it had something to do with the emptiness of the courtyard, the silence faintly

15

humming with air conditioners, the still water, perhaps that the only person he had seen in the hotel was a desk clerk in jacket and trousers that matched the color scheme.

The red glow flipped through the air, turning circles like a dud Roman candle, and fizzled into the pool. A guy in white shorts and a dark polo shirt came out of somewhere and walked toward the deck chair waving his arm at the cigarette in the pool. Their voices sounded like a muffled scrape of metal. She stood up, and Wilson could see her then, finally, not bad, in a white one-piece bathing suit. She walked with what seemed like an exaggerated sway, perhaps swinging a drink in her hand, past the man in shorts, who turned as she passed, still grumbling, and lumbered after her.

After that the courtyard was empty and uninteresting. Wilson took a pint bottle of Cutty Sark out of his suitcase and poured out a long shot into a plastic glass he had found wrapped in cellophane in the bathroom. The television squatted in the corner like a familiar fat guest. It was the kind of room that scared him sometimes. There was a little round tin on the floor in the corner, which looked like a tin of snuff and said ANT TRAP on the top. There was a small opening at the front of it, and he imagined that inside there was a chemical that attracted ants and another chemical that poisoned them. There didn't appear to be any ants around to try it.

The next night Haeflinger had taken him to a bar in Chicago, one of those dark joints with sawdust on the floor full of men in business suits talking business and telling dirty stories. Women were seldom seen there and had in fact been barred by the management until the practice was declared unconstitutional. It was the kind of place Haeflinger liked. He was a big man with spiky gray hairs coming out of his nose and ears. He had been in the detective business for a long time and had accumulated a lot of information, which he wouldn't talk about unless he was drunk. So when he wanted to brief an agent he invited him for drinks. It was a Freudian thing, somebody had said once, like guys who can't have sex unless they're a little loaded.

"This Dantry son of a bitch," Haeflinger growled, halfway through his second bourbon, "wants to go into politics. That's why he's nervous about this thing. So we gotta play it real careful, see?"

Wilson grunted and looked down the barrel of his drink. Haeflinger got drunk quickly and then maintained the same level of drunkenness more or less indefinitely. He scooped up a big handful of peanuts and squinted into Wilson's face.

"He show you his pictures?"

"No," Wilson said, "he showed me his buffalo head."

Haeflinger laughed with a nasty, braying sound and choked on a peanut skin. He coughed horribly and took a swallow of whiskey.

"Yeah, I seen it," he said hoarsely when he had recovered, and shouted at the bartender, a dour-looking Filipino called Jimmy. It was the kind of bar where the customers derive some peculiar satisfaction from calling the bartender by name.

"I mean *his* pictures," Haeflinger went on, "You know, art. He's got this collection in his house in Colorado, in the cellar."

Wilson shook his head. He didn't have any interest in hearing about Dantry's art collection. He imagined Indian braves staring at sunsets. Things like that.

"It's all stuff from the fifteenth, sixteenth century. That's what he likes. Italian stuff, Rembrandt and Dante and guys like that."

Dante, Wilson thought. Dante?

"It's like a fucking museum," Haeflinger said, rattling the ice in the fresh glass Jimmy had set in front of him. "And the thing is, most of the stuff's stolen. You know what I mean?"

"No," Wilson said. "What d'you mean?"

"Stolen," Haeflinger said, putting his face a little closer to Wilson's. "Somebody stole them from somewhere. Museums, private collections . . . Where do you think they sell stuff like that? To rich guys like Dantry that want it bad enough to pay good money for it and keep their mouths shut."

"Uh-huh," Wilson said. He didn't particularly like Haeflinger, had never liked him, drunk or sober, but it was true what they said: You could always learn something having a drink with him.

"You know what the son of a bitch said to me? He showed me the collection. We had some business—matter of verifying the authenticity of a piece—that's a little difficult with stolen goods."

Haeflinger grinned, squinting up his left eye. "Good client, Dantry. You do a good job on this, right? And be careful." Haeflinger took another drink and shook his head. "What was I telling you? Oh, yeah. What he said to me. He said, 'You know, I don't really

17

give that much of a shit about art. I just like owning things nobody else can have.' You get it?"

It hadn't seemed particularly important, but it was the sort of thing you remembered. Wilson wiped the grease off his fingers with a paper napkin, drank some more beer, and watched the waterfall on the beer sign for a while. Elizabeth Dantry had both elbows on the bar and an empty look on her face. Pretty soon the bar was going to close, and there was the question of what they were going to do then. Sleep, Wilson thought, but he didn't really believe it. The voice on the jukebox said:

> *Once upon a time there was light in my life,*
> *Now there's only love in the dark . . .*

4

The city of Barcelona is widely believed to have been named after the Carthaginian general Hamilcar Barca, father of the more famous Hannibal, who is supposed to have passed through as well, with his elephants on his way to fight the Romans in Italy, where he seems to have won all the battles but lost the war. On the other hand, certain authorities claim that Hamilcar Barca had nothing to do with the naming of Barcelona. Looking down from the airplane, it hadn't seemed to make any difference either way.

Wilson had seen a deep-blue sea curling into a concrete shore, a sky of silvery blue that hurt his eyes, the city sprawled interminably along a jagged coastline, straggling off into hills of brown and green. The plane came down fast, circled, swung in past the usual stuff—long low buildings and expanses of concrete steaming in the sun—and hit the ground with a bump. It was morning then, a little after midnight according to Wilson's watch, because when you fly east you move forward in time, strangely enough. You're in the future before you know it, you've lost six hours and you're not sure how you're going to get them back.

It was hot when he walked down the metal stairway off the

19

were a couple of Impressionist prints, a bookshelf with some Spanish grammars, and a book called *I'm Okay, You're Okay.*

"She ever bring guys home with her? At night, I mean."

"Sometimes," she said in a half whisper, avoiding his eyes. The walls looked thin as any other apartment house walls, Wilson thought. He imagined her waking up and listening to them screw. She probably knew what he was imagining, and she didn't like it.

"Did you ever meet any of these guys?"

"No."

Wilson sighed, thought about taking out his pipe and decided she wouldn't like it. "What about her mail? What'd she tell you to do with her mail?"

She took a quick look around the room and said, "She said there wouldn't be any mail." It wasn't very convincing.

"Look, Miss Walters," Wilson said, "you're not really being much help, you know. You realize Elizabeth could be in some kind of trouble?"

"Elizabeth's not in any trouble," Marjorie said sharply. "She's just doing what she wants. Like she always does."

"You're pretty sure about that?"

"That's the way she is."

He waited for her to go on, but she left it at that.

"So what'd she do to you?" he said. "Steal your boyfriend?"

She just sat there staring at him with her face lit up and a miserable expression, and after a while he closed up his little notebook and put it back in his pocket. She was lying about a few things, but it hadn't seemed important enough to get nasty about, because he guessed she was probably telling the truth about the main thing: that it was just a case of some little rich girl fucking around.

"You think you're so God damn smart," the blond woman said slowly, her voice brutally loud in the quiet after the bartender had turned the jukebox off. When she finished there was no sound but the hum of the air-conditioning and the grumble of the refrigerators. The guy in the plaid shirt looked as if he was going to say something, then he just hunched down over his beer.

The bartender came around behind the bar and said, "Closing time, folks," and turned off the waterfall on the beer sign.

22

Wilson paid and looked at Elizabeth. She seemed washed out and far away, but she slid off the barstool and they walked out without a word. Outside the air was cool and smelled of desert.

She shook her head when Wilson offered to drive and got in behind the wheel. It was her car, he thought, she could probably make the couple hundred yards to the motel without hitting anything. There wasn't much around to hit.

It took about two minutes to get there, time enough for her to find a rock 'n' roll station coming out of Salt Lake City or Reno, someplace way out there in the dark. Choruses of winged insects were fluttering suicidally around the two lights that cast a dusty yellow glow over the five or six cars in the lot. Wilson made out two sets of head and shoulders in the front seat of one of them, a Dodge, not close together, just sitting there doing nothing at half-past two in the morning. He put his hand on her sleeve and felt her flinch, felt the thinness of her arm through the cloth.

"Hold it," he said softly.

The brakes squealed when she hit them, gravel churned under the tires. The two heads seemed to turn, and then Wilson heard the car start. He tried to figure out what that would mean, but nothing came. Too much beer, too much dope. It was already too late anyway.

She slammed into reverse, twitched the rear end around, slid the Ford out onto the highway, and put the pedal to the floor. "Turn it up," she said.

"Huh?" Wilson said, twisting around to look out the back window.

"The radio," she said. "I like this song."

"Take that road to the left," he said. He hoped she could do it before they hit the highway. He didn't want her to try to outrun them. He didn't even want to think about it.

She flipped the volume up with one finger just before she hit the brake, and a funky saxophone blasted out as she turned. She had a little grin at the corners of her mouth and she didn't look drunk anymore. She was good, Wilson thought. Her daddy probably gave her a Porsche to play around with when she was sixteen. He saw the front end of the Dodge lurching out and said, "Cut the lights."

The car hit the side road with a slam in the dark and shimmied for a moment before she straightened it out. She edged it forward carefully then, feeling for the road. Wilson, watching the back window, reached for the purse on the seat beside her and pulled it toward him, feeling the weight of the automatic inside. He couldn't see the highway then, but he knew that if they had seen them turn they would have been there already. Of course they could still come back. There was a moon and an infinity of stars. You could more or less make out the road when your eyes got used to the dark. He turned off the radio. He sensed rather than really saw clapboard houses and house trailers out there in the dark, anybody's guess what the hell people did around there. No point in waking up the neighbors.

"You might as well turn on the parking lights now," he said. "They must have thought we stayed on the highway."

She drove a little faster with the low beams on, lighting up scrubby dry weeds along the side of the road. It was stupid, Wilson thought. They would have a fast car and they would figure out what had happened pretty quickly, and then they would be back. There were only two ways to go and neither of them were any good.

She took a cigarette from the pack on the dashboard and offered him the pack.

He shook his head. "This isn't going to work, you know."

She wasn't grinning anymore. When she lit the cigarette her face looked weary and fixed like a mask in the glow from her lighter.

"You know who those guys are?" Wilson said.

She blew out some smoke and shrugged, keeping her eyes on the road. After a minute she stopped the car. It was quiet, a funny kind of quiet, not even any crickets.

"You might as well get out now," she said. "You can walk back to the hotel. I don't suppose it's very far."

"I couldn't do that," Wilson said. He could make out the shape of her purse against her hip. He hadn't noticed her take it back. It looked as if she had her hand inside it.

"You can just tell 'em you had a beer with me," she said. "You can tell 'em whatever you want. What *do* you want, anyway?"

Wilson stuffed some tobacco into the bowl of his pipe and wished he could think a little faster.

"We keep on going this way, we'll run into 'em again sooner or later," he said.

"I'm not going back," she said flatly.

"Where the hell do you think you are going?" Wilson said. There was something ridiculously futile about talking to her, but when they didn't talk they seemed to be in a vast empty bowl of silence, just sitting there waiting for something to happen.

"I don't care," she said. She took the empty cigarette pack off the dashboard, crumpled it, and dropped it over the back of the seat. "I wouldn't tell you anyway."

Wilson lit his pipe for the second time, sucking on it till he was puffing out billowy clouds of smoke. His mouth was already raw from too much smoking. He didn't feel too good in general.

"We could go back to the motel," he said between puffs, "park behind it. I could get my car. They don't know me, they don't know the car. Leave this one here."

It didn't seem like a particularly brilliant idea, but it was the only idea he had. She looked at him without expression for so long he started thinking that she had fallen asleep with her eyes open. They would be back any time, Wilson thought. He heard a semi roaring down the highway, he thought he heard the sound of a car behind it. She still had her hand inside the purse.

"You can get my stuff out of the room, okay?" she said finally, switching on the ignition.

5

They drove around quietly on the dirt roads until they could see the lights over the motel parking lot and the stretch of highway beyond it, like a dead snake under the lights. They stopped and Wilson got out, closing the door gently behind him. There was nothing but a dark empty field between him and the back of the motel.

"Stay here, okay?" Wilson said.

She nodded and opened up another pack of cigarettes.

The moon helped a little, not much. The ground was bluish and irregular, dotted with lumpish shapes that were unrecognizable until he was almost on top of them. He imagined things underfoot, dead animals and live ones, rusty bear traps . . .

He came around the side of the building, looked over the lot, and saw that his car was still in the same place. The Dodge wasn't there, and it was quiet except for a radio muttering in the office and the bugs beating their wings on the lights. Wilson hitched up his trousers and walked down to the room.

They had forced the door and gone over the room in a hurry. Wilson checked that the curtains were closed, shut the door, and blundered across to the bedside light and turned it on. Elizabeth's things were scattered around, and they had pulled out all the drawers in the little plywood dresser. The one where she had put Wilson's gun was empty, like all the others. He shrugged and started gathering up her clothes and jamming them into the suitcase. He wasn't very good at packing anyway, and every time he heard something on the road he felt a tingling in his arms.

He closed the suitcase and turned out the light, opened the door, and stood there for a second with the suitcase in his hand looking out. It didn't look any different. The gravel made a crunching sound underfoot as he crossed the lot, but nobody seemed to notice. When he got in the car he recognized the familiar smells of pipe tobacco and marijuana and another, more subtle odor that was probably his own sweat. He started the car and wondered for just a moment what he was doing. They should have been back by then, he thought, and then he thought maybe they were.

He wound around the back roads until he found the place. The yellow Ford was still there, but there didn't look like there was anybody in it when he pulled up behind. He got out and walked over. He couldn't hear any cars, or anything else, for that matter. He thought he saw something move out in the dark to his right, something small and fast.

She was stretched out across the front seat with her head against the passenger door and her eyes closed. He tapped on the window once and then again a little louder. Her head moved, she opened her eyes and stared at him and then sat up. Wilson opened the door.

"Let's go," he said in a whisper. "I got your stuff."

She nodded vaguely, rubbed her forehead, and pushed the hair back off her face. She was still half asleep, Wilson thought, with no defenses. When she looked at him again she looked as if she knew what he was thinking.

"Yeah," she said, "let's go."

She went back to sleep almost at once when they got back on the highway. Wilson kept his eye on the rearview mirror as he drove and tried to remember when the next junction would be coming up. He figured to take it, wherever it happened to go, figured any variation helped their odds. He thought about smoking a joint but decided against it. A joint could wake you up, distract you for

27

awhile, just like a drink, or maybe a little better, but if you smoked too much or if you were too tired to begin with it had the opposite effect. And it wasn't a good idea to smoke when you were scared. The world just got big and scary and meaningless, and there wasn't any scenery to look at at the moment, just the line down the middle of the road. He remembered a song, called "White Line Fever," about the white line down the middle of the highway. He tried humming it to himself for awhile but he couldn't remember the tune.

He turned on the radio and listened to disco music fading out in the distance for a while. The disc jockey started talking about a steakhouse a long way away and Wilson realized he was hungry. He turned left at the junction and headed north. When he switched off the radio Elizabeth woke up. She sat for a while staring out at the road, not saying anything, with her purse against her hip.

"Where we going?" she said finally.

"You wanta go to Los Angeles, right?"

"How do you know?"

Wilson shrugged. "It figures."

"What's your game?"

"I haven't got a game. I'm much too tired to play."

She said, "Sure," as if she didn't believe it at all, and rested her head on the back of the seat. They sat there without saying anything, and the dark ripped past the windows.

"How about if you tell me what happened over there?" Wilson said. He kept his eyes on the road, tried to make his voice sound casual. He wasn't sure he had succeeded.

"It's a long story."

"I'm not in any hurry."

She reached for her cigarettes and put her feet up on the dashboard in front of her.

"I suppose it started with Ramon."

"Ramon?"

"Ramon Munet. I guess you don't know him."

"Yeah," Wilson said, "I talked to Munet."

She glanced over at him and blew out some smoke. "I guess you talked to lots of people about me, didn't you?"

Wilson shrugged. "I don't know," he muttered.

"Did you talk to Marjorie?"

"Yeah."

"What did she say?"

"She said you didn't wash your dishes."

Elizabeth chuckled. "Poor Marjorie," she said. That cheered her up a little.

"So what about Munet?" Wilson said after a minute.

"I guess he was the first man I got involved with that wasn't really a kid. He was a good lover too. He paid attention, you know what I mean?"

"Uhm," Wilson said. He had the feeling he would have blushed if they hadn't been in the dark. Funny how people don't blush in the dark.

"But he was just playing games. Like everybody else. Juanjo too, I guess. So the joke was on me."

6

The university was empty in July, and the building Wilson had been directed to had the trashed-out look of a New York apartment block in one of those movies that take place after a nuclear war. He wandered around for quite awhile before he found an office that was open, and the one secretary seemed happy to have the chance to talk to anybody. It took her some time to find anything on Elizabeth, but eventually she came up with a notation of payment made in April to audit a course given by a certain Adolfo Merino Grau. He had an office on the third floor, the secretary said. It was possible he was there, but not very likely.

There were three names on the door, Merino's on the top. Wilson knocked twice and thought he heard a kind of murmur from inside after the second knock and pushed open the door. Inside there were three desks, a few chairs and shelves, a blue carpet. A little man in a blue suit was apparently asleep in a swivel chair, his white hair like a fluffy halo in the sunlight slanting in the open window.

Wilson cleared his throat and the little man straightened up quickly, picked up a pen, and peered severely at the papers on top of his desk before looking up.

"Excuse me," Wilson said. "I'm looking for Professor Merino."

"Dr. Merino," the little man corrected, and smiled. "I'm Merino. No doubt you are not familiar with our nomenclature. Your Spanish is excellent. I gather from your accent that you are North American?"

"That's right."

Merino smiled again, evidently pleased with his accuracy, and long wrinkles showed around his eyes. He had pale, parchmenty skin and a little bird's head on a skinny neck. "What can I do for you? Please sit down."

"I'm looking for information about a girl named Elizabeth Dantry," Wilson said, taking a chair. "I was told she took one of your classes this spring."

"Elizabeth Dantry?" Merino repeated. He shook his head and raised his hands in a gesture of helplessness. "There are so many."

"American girl. She audited your course on the, uh . . . picaresque novel."

"Ah," Merino said, raising one finger, "Ramon Munet's friend perhaps?"

"I don't know," Wilson said. "An American girl?"

"Yes, I think perhaps she was American, something like that."

"So you remember her?"

"Oh, no." Merino chuckled. "There were sixty or seventy in that class. Of course I don't remember them." He sighed and folded his hands. They were long and white, crisscrossed with bluish veins.

"This is a factory, you see. Our task is to produce an intellectual type that has become sufficiently accustomed to absurdity to spend the rest of its life reproducing it. They learn, for example, to develop a completely uninteresting idea over several hundred pages on the assumption that most attention will be paid to the footnotes. The sophists have won, definitively. The ancient Greeks would have pulled their robes over their heads, turned their faces to the wall, and died. Or perhaps it was the Romans. But we are not the ancient Greeks, are we? Are you interested in rats, Mr. . . . ?"

"Wilson," Wilson said. "Rats?"

"Those experiments they do with rats. I never have been myself. I have always thought that the analogy did not apply. Rats are rats, and my fellow professors . . ."

31

His face lit up with a brief, mischievous smile, and then he went on, gazing brightly into Wilson's face. "Apparently there is some sort of pleasure center in the rat's brain, and in mine, and in yours. In their experiments they have attached electrodes to these centers that stimulate them, producing a sensation of pleasure when activated. The rats were taught to operate the device themselves by working a lever of some sort. It appears that once they had learned many of them employed it almost constantly, to the extent that they neglected to eat and eventually starved. What do you think that means?"

"I don't know," Wilson said.

"Neither do I," Merino said, looking out the window with a bemused expression. He might have forgotten Wilson was there, or perhaps it was just not very important to him.

"So who's this Ramon Munet?" Wilson said after a minute.

"Munet?" Merino's lips curled briefly into an expression of mild distaste. "A brilliant young man. Well, he's not very young any more. Theater director, rather avant-garde, I understand. Not my field."

"But Elizabeth was—or is, rather—a friend of his?"

"If it's the same girl. I remember a girl brought me a note from Munet. I believe she was foreign. I don't really remember if I ever saw her again. What I remember was Munet sending me the silly note. She could have spoken to me herself, of course. In Barcelona, you see, everyone knows everyone else, whether they want to or not."

"Do you happen to have his address?" Wilson said.

"Somewhere perhaps," Merino said vaguely, "but I imagine he would be on the coast now. At this time of year the cream of our intellectual society can be found on the Costa Brava and similar places, cultivating their suntans."

He paused to smile beatifically. "Stuffing themselves with champagne and oysters and gazing wistfully at young girls' bodies."

So Wilson had phoned Munet's home and gotten the name of the town on the coast where Munet was staying from someone who was probably the cleaning lady, rented a Ford Fiesta and driven north out of Barcelona on the motorway toward the Costa Brava. He had done the usual things by then, checked the hospitals, the police, the passenger lists at the airport. She could have left by train or bus, of course, and there was no way to check that. She could have been kidnapped or she could be dead. Or she could be sitting in a living room a couple of doors down the street watching the afternoon movie on TV. She could have disappeared without a trace, but that didn't happen very often. There wasn't anything to worry about in any case. Haeflinger wrote a good contract. Whatever condition she was in when they found her, they would collect, plus expenses. So there wasn't any hurry.

And it wasn't that hard to find people usually. Wilson had found two or three in his time, Haeflinger had probably found hundreds. It wasn't that hard, maybe because most people really wanted somebody to find them.

He drove past rows of fortresslike apartment buildings with laundry on the balconies, and then there were dry hills, a little river in the valley below with a brewery beside it. The green got deeper the farther he got from the city, and when he left the motorway to take the highway to the coast he could see pine forests edging up into blue mountains, fields of sunflowers along the road.

Wilson took his time driving and smoked a joint. There were villages every few miles, of rough stone houses with tile roofs, gently rolling fields and woodlands. He turned onto a secondary road, and then he saw something dark and bloody at the center of the pavement. He swerved around it, and looking at its prickly gray and brown fur and its little pointed snout, he guessed it must have been a hedgehog. He didn't think he had ever seen one except in illustrations in children's books. It was smashed in a pool of dark, fresh-looking blood, and the sight of it gave him an abrupt sick sensation. He gripped the wheel, and for a while after that the car engine sounded loud and rattly. He felt as if he were sitting in a tin box, and the trees and fields moving past looked distant and not quite real.

The road was steep and winding down to the sea, and Wilson, wrestling the car around the curves, felt a kind of childish excitement when he began to catch glimpses of it, sparkling way down below through the pines. The place was not really a village, just a pebbly beach, a hotel, and a cluster of little houses, with more houses terracing the slopes around the small cove. Wilson parked on the edge of the beach and got out. It was late afternoon and there were not many people, and even the children didn't make much

33

noise. There were old wooden fishing boats drawn up on the stones to one side and a few small pleasure crafts. Wilson walked over to the terrace in front of the hotel, sat down at a metal table, and took out his pipe.

A waitress in a crisp beige uniform pointed Munet's place out to him when she served him his beer, a white stucco house with a chocolate-brown roof and a little terrace in front, halfway up the hillside. Wilson drank his beer slowly, smoking and watching the water slide gently up over the pebbles. He wondered what it would be like to live in a place like that. He didn't think he was likely to find out. According to his calculations, his pension would give him about enough to retire to a crappy little house in one of the Chicago suburbs, with a three-by-five garden to water when he got bored with watching TV.

He was sweaty and puffing a little from the climb when he got to Munet's house. Not even forty-five and you're out of shape and thinking about your pension, he thought disgustedly. The floor of the terrace was smooth reddish stone. There were two canvas chairs and a round white table with a glass ashtray on it, a cigarette butt in the ashtray that looked as if it had been there for a long time. Munet came out before he had the chance to knock, looked at him and raised his eyebrows. He was wearing a soft yachtsman's cap, black swimming trunks and a polo shirt. He was tan, with thick dark hair sprinkled with gray and the beginning of a pot belly coming out over the waistband of his trunks.

"My name's Wilson," Wilson said. "I'm looking for Elizabeth Dantry."

Munet frowned and shook his head. "She isn't here."

"Are you Ramon Munet?"

"Yes. What's the problem?"

"Elizabeth's apparently disappeared. Her father sent me to find her."

Munet looked at him with a certain interest, nodded. "I haven't seen her for some time."

"I see," Wilson said, and shifted his weight from one leg to the other.

"Sit down," Munet said, waving at a chair. It was the kind of low canvas chair that you have to lower yourself into carefully and

34

that isn't easy to get out of. "Would you like a drink? A sherry?"

"Fine," Wilson said insincerely. Sherry to him was the kind of thing his aunts used to drink at Christmastime. He filled his pipe and lit it and tried unsuccessfully to throw the match over the edge of the terrace. There was a nice view. The sea changed color farther out, to a deeper blue, and there were sailboats.

Munet brought out two slim glasses of sherry and set them on the table. He sat down and they took simultaneous ceremonial sips.

"A very intelligent girl, Elizabeth," Munet said, "with a lot of vitality, curiosity, and, I suppose, a certain capacity for self-destruction."

"Why do you say that?"

Munet waved a hand vaguely. "Attitudes," he said, and frowned at the sea. He had what people call a distinguished profile. He probably knew that.

"When did you last see her?"

"Some time ago, as I said."

"In Barcelona?"

"No. In a forest."

He paused, glancing at Wilson out of the corner of his eye as if to check if he had achieved the desired effect, and then went on. "I had organized an experience, an intensive open workshop to be held in an isolated area. Absolutely no contact with anyone outside the group, no telephones, no radio, no music except the music we could make ourselves. The concept . . . well, it's not an entirely original idea of course. Grotowski took a group to a place in Africa. It's a rather well-known story."

He glanced inquiringly at Wilson and Wilson shook his head. He hadn't heard the story. He had the impression that he might have heard of this Grotowski, but maybe it was Bukowski, a Polish garbageman who wrote dirty stories about being a garbageman.

"Grotowski wanted to take his people into an extremely isolated area inhabited by a tribe of Bushmen, and in order to do so he had to get the permission of the tribe. The tribe discussed the matter and decided to let them in—except Grotowski. They said he was a white devil."

Munet smiled and took another symbolic sip of sherry. "Gro-

35

towski does look quite diabolical, if you've ever seen a picture of him."

Munet fell silent for a moment, thinking about something. There were certain advantages, Wilson thought, to talking in front of a view. You talked into it and shut up when you ran out of things to say. It was more relaxed that way.

"We were quite comfortable, we had plenty of food, wine, sleeping bags, tents—though some preferred to make their dwellings out of fallen branches and stones. There was no program. The idea was quite simple. We were going to improvise, for two weeks. The idea, the concept, was that the actor is not just expression, he is experience. Or, if you like, in order to express he must experience, his capacity for experience must be deepened and intensified, made flexible and spontaneous. He has to learn to lose himself. He has, in a word, to learn how to play."

Munet paused, smiling faintly with modest satisfaction. Wilson, puffing on his pipe, felt pleasantly drowsy with the sun and the sherry. Munet had an actor's voice and he knew how to play it. It didn't particularly matter what he said.

"There was makeup and material for costumes. We invented characters and changed them when we felt like it, and this went on day and night. It was like learning to be like children again in a way, rediscovering the pleasure of losing oneself in fantasy. It was an extraordinary experience really, and the place was extraordinary. You began to feel the forest around you like a living thing. It was all fantasy, play, but it seemed at times more real than anything I have ever experienced."

Munet stroked his nose meditatively, his voice went a little lower and took on a melancholy languor. "I remembered when I was a child playing in the late afternoon when it was getting dark—in the autumn, I suppose, when it gets dark early—and being so involved in my games that when I was called to come in it seemed like something precious and irreplaceable was being taken from me, and it was terrible because I knew then that those moments would be lost forever. There, in the forest, there was no one to call us in."

Munet cleared his throat and looked at Wilson severely, with a certain embarassment, as if it had just occurred to him that a fat American detective might not know what he was talking about.

36

"There were about twenty-five people in the group," he said dully, looking out across the cove at the trees opposite. "Elizabeth expressed an interest, so I arranged for her to come. I suppose it was a mistake."

"Why?"

"It's difficult to explain really. She wasn't prepared for the experience. Because in fact we were not children, and there was nothing childish about what we were doing."

He looked vaguely at Wilson's empty glass and took a sip of his own. "The demonic element has been part of the theater since its beginnings, since the goat dance of the Greeks or before. The Church knew that, which is why they tried to suppress it and in the mystery plays turned the devil into a figure of fun. When Artaud proposed his catharsis through terror he was only signaling a return to Dionysian origins, in which in contrast to the distancing of Aristotle's pity and horror, spectacle becomes ritual once again, and the public is the enemy, to be annihilated and devoured. The audience becomes part of the ritual or it simply ceases to count. The impressions of the critic as spokesman for the passive spectator are of no more interest than the last moments of the Christmas turkey."

He paused, more for effect than for breath, and Wilson imagined him sitting around his little house, working this stuff around in his head and writing it down on little bits of paper.

"The modern theater is the only place in the world where the savage and the madman rule, where the bourgeoisie—or the masses, it's the same now, isn't it?—pay to be bullied and humiliated by their clowns. Perhaps it isn't necessary for the actor to be a demon, but he must be a kind of intelligent savage. And all savages have their demons."

Wilson scraped out his pipe into the ashtray with a matchstick. The shadows were getting longer and the sunlight had turned a wispy gold. People on the beach were picking up their towels and suntan oils and straggling up to the tin tables in front of the hotel to have drinks and eat potato chips.

"So what happened?" Wilson said.

Munet blinked at him. "A great many things happened," he said mildly.

"I mean with Elizabeth."

Munet shook his head. "I don't think Elizabeth really understood what we were doing. Americans tend to be rather literal minded, don't they?"

Wilson shrugged. It wasn't something he had ever thought about.

"And perhaps she was frightened."

"Of what?"

Munet sighed. "What happened," he said slowly, "was more or less what I supposed would happen, though I didn't know exactly how. It was an experiment, you see, for me, for all of us, and to me an experiment is of no interest if you know from the beginning how it is going to come out. I personally believe—I am with the Romantics on this—in art as a path of discovery, a means to the acquisition of knowledge, and that means that the experience of the artist may be at least as important as his work. To him at least. There are perhaps certain things he wants to know, or only to feel, only once perhaps, in order to have experienced, to know what you are, what you might have been, what you have been even if only for an instant. And the performances or the paintings or the books are like shells, like memories of this experience, a kind of pale shadow that remains. Do you understand what I mean?"

"Not really," Wilson said, "but it doesn't matter."

Munet frowned, pinched the bridge of his nose, and looked out to sea. The deep blue was coming closer to the shore. Perhaps that was the tide, Wilson thought, or maybe just a trick of the light.

"But Elizabeth isn't an artist," Munet said finally.

"Did she think she was?"

"They all do, don't they?" Munet said dryly.

Wilson lit his pipe again and smoked for a moment. Then he said, "Go on," with a certain impatience in his voice.

"It was always at night," Munet said quietly, "I mean everything happened at night. Finally there was something . . . like something I've read about. The return, the celebration of the primal chaos. There was plenty of wine, and there were drugs, of course there were drugs. Some of them started going around naked, and then they painted their bodies with phosphorescent paint, started beating on hollow logs or cans, screaming, and it spread, the madness spread, until it was as if everyone had gone mad and you had to go mad too, or . . ."

"And then you had an orgy," Wilson said.

Munet glanced at him coldly and said, "If you like."

"Were you lovers, you and Elizabeth?"

Munet shifted on his chair and folded his hands on his belly. "There's a kind of university student that tends to get involved . . . It's awkward sometimes. A girl like Laura . . ."

"Elizabeth," Wilson corrected, "we're talking about Elizabeth."

"Yes," Munet said quickly, "girls like Elizabeth tend to get very involved, and she was out of place. It wasn't a goddam camping trip."

"Did she come back with you?"

"She left before it was finished."

"Before or after the orgy?"

"After," Munet said.

"What date would that be?"

"We didn't have dates there," Munet said irritably. "Three or four days before we came back. That was on the twenty-seventh of May."

"Have you seen her since?"

"You talk like a cop, you know that?"

"Yeah," Wilson said indifferently, "I suppose I do."

"I talked to her on the phone," Munet said after a minute.

"When was that?"

"Some time in June, I suppose," Munet said tiredly.

"What did you talk about?"

"I thought . . . I wondered if she was all right. I wanted to let her know that . . . I was there."

"What did she say?"

"Nothing much as far as I can remember."

It was that time of the afternoon when the air gets a little cooler, and the silence had a deep, languid quality. It was nice there, Wilson thought.

"What's happened to her exactly?" Munet said.

"She moved out of the place where she was living and didn't say where she was going, she hasn't been in touch with her parents,

39

and she hasn't picked up her allowance. Maybe she's just sort of run away from home. You think she'd do something like that?"

"I don't know," Munet said thoughtfully. "Her parents must have money—to send you here, I mean."

"Yeah. Do you remember any particular friends Elizabeth made on this . . . ah, excursion?"

"Nobody in particular," Munet said glumly. "There's a list. For the students it was half a credit. I suppose I could give you a copy if you like."

"I'd appreciate that," Wilson said.

Lights were beginning to come on in the dusk, in the hotel and the little houses around the cove, when Wilson got to his car. He drove up the winding road from the sea and got lost for a while in a tangle of dark roads before he found the town where the woman at his hotel in Barcelona had made him a reservation. There were kids riding up and down the main street on the edge of the beach on small, noisy motorcycles and people strolling after their showers. The hotel dining room seemed to be full of German families with long-legged blond children. He ate an indifferent dinner and drank half a bottle of wine. Then he walked along the beach for a while, watching the waves break on the rocks, ate an ice cream cone, and went to bed.

7

Wilson saw the cluster of lights when it was still far off across the dark plain and watched it spread out slowly in front of him as he got closer. Elizabeth slept, her head tilted against the window, and he could make out the softly blurred outline of her face in the glow from the dashboard when he glanced over. The engine made a steady, humming growl, and the road was straight and empty except for the occasional semi that boomed by like a kind of arrogant mechanical monster. The buzz from the beer had worn off by then and left him tired and sad and perhaps a little shaky. He wanted coffee and food.

The lights broke up into scattered dots that threw a thin glow over sleeping shapes. There were a few old signs along the road that he didn't bother to read, the name of the town that he forgot almost as soon as he had read it. The highway turned into Main Street and ran past flimsy frame houses with withered lawns and rusty-looking cars parked in front, a white Dairy Queen stand in the middle of an empty lot, a Woolworth's and a bank, all closed up tight. When he stopped at a stop sign an Indian sitting on the post office step tried to stand up, put one hand on the wall, and got halfway up and then sat down again, shaking his head.

At the other end of town there was a restaurant with a gold ball on a pillar shaped like a golf tee out in front. The gold ball was turning slowly, and the neon sign said SMITTY's 24 HOURS. As he turned into the parking lot Wilson suddenly envisioned a fat cop with a cowboy hat and a .45 on his hip walking in on them while they were eating their pancakes. He tried to calculate the chances that they had put out a make on his car, and realized that he was too tired to care. He felt Elizabeth stirring and muttered, "Get something to eat."

The restaurant had the kind of bright lights that make everything under them look ugly. There was a long counter and booths covered in yellow plastic along the big windows that looked out onto the street, so that you could watch the cars go by if there had been any. Elizabeth went to the toilet, and Wilson slid awkwardly into the booth, opened the menu, and looked at the colored photos of stacks of pancakes and plates of ham and eggs.

The waitress came over and said, "Good morning," without a trace of sarcasm, poured them some coffee and went away. She was wearing a short, pleated uniform with a little white apron and a lot of strawberry lipstick, and she had a frazzled smile that she turned off and on. A couple of old men in cowboy hats were drinking coffee in another booth and yelling at each other in slow dry voices, and a drunk was sitting at the counter with his chin sinking slowly toward the dish of apple pie in front of him. It was the kind of place Wilson remembered sitting in all night when he was a kid, getting high on cup after cup of lousy coffee and listening to the piped-in music. It made you feel grown up, for some reason.

Elizabeth had washed her face and put on some makeup around her eyes, but it didn't make her look much happier. She poked at a club sandwich with her fork, drank coffee, and smoked cigarettes while Wilson ate ham and eggs with hash brown potatoes and toast. It felt strange sitting across from her under all that light. Like a couple on a blind date that wasn't working out.

Wilson excused himself when he had finished eating, walked around the edge of the counter and into the little passage where there was a telephone on the wall outside the toilets. He had thought that there might be. He went through the swinging door into the men's room, urinated, and washed his hands and face. Then he stood in front of the mirror for a moment, poked his stomach with a forefinger and felt it bounce back. An old man in a baseball cap and running shoes shuffled out of the corner stall and squinted up at Wilson with little bleary eyes.

"I can't sleep," he said. "I can't sleep worth a damn."

"That's tough," Wilson said sympathetically.

"What the hell would you know about it?" the old guy said, and shuffled out.

Wilson put all the change he had on the shelf under the phone, dialed the prefix for Chicago, and started on the office number. There wouldn't be anybody there, but he could leave a message on the answering machine. He looked up and she was standing a few feet away from him with her purse over her shoulder and her hand inside it. She looked quite professional, he thought.

"What are you doing?" she said.

"I've gotta call my boss."

"Put it down."

Wilson hesitated, and the phone started making a bleeping noise in his ear.

"He'll just tell your father where you are," he said.

"I don't want my father to know where I am."

"Why not?"

"Because I don't trust him. I don't trust you either."

One of the cowboys edged around her, wobbling on his boot heels, and said, " 'Scuse me," as he went into the men's room.

"Put it down," she said again.

Wilson rested his arm on the shelf, holding the bleeping phone, trying to look relaxed. "What're you gonna do, shoot me?"

She would maybe. She looked serious enough about the whole thing, she was worn out, hyped up on poisonous restaurant coffee. People saw characters shooting one another so often in the movies that they got to wondering what it felt like. The phone was getting sweaty in his hand, and the bleeps were beginning to get on his nerves. He smiled unconvincingly and hung up the phone.

"Now gimme the keys," she said.

43

Wilson shook his head. "Who the hell do you think you are," he said, "Calamity Jane?"

She stared at him for a second and then started to giggle. "Calamity Jane?" she said.

8

Wilson opened his eyes slowly, and the expanding band of light before him looked something like the first tropical dawn on the first day of creation. As his eyes began to focus strips of color formed a beach, sea, and sky and pale blobs became almost naked bodies speckled with sweat and smears of suntan oil. The glare off the sea hurt his eyes, his body felt sticky with sweat and sand clung to his legs. He became gradually aware of a voice from above mispronouncing his name and saw black trousers rising out of the sand at his feet, turning into a waiter somewhere between himself and the excruciatingly blue sky.

"Telephone, Mr. Wilson," the waiter said, waving a hand at the hotel behind Wilson's head. His black trousers looked uncomfortable and slightly ridiculous surrounded by all that bare flesh, and he looked as if he knew it.

Wilson sat up, squinting, rubbed his chest and muttered something, and the waiter trudged off, his black shoes making big holes in the sand. Wilson gathered up his towel, newspaper, and sandals and made his way past the bodies and paraphernalia laid out on the sand, past the tables on the terrace where people sat under striped awnings staring patiently out at the sea as if they expected something to rise out of it at any moment, and into the hotel bar. The darkness was impenetrable at first after the brightness outside. Then he made out a waiter pointing at a telephone at the end of the bar. It was a red telephone, the receiver laying on its side, and to Wilson, still groggy after sleeping in the sun, it had a strangely repulsive, hostile look to it. He licked his lips, tasting the salt on them, and asked the waiter for a beer. Then he picked up the phone and said hello.

"Wilson? Where the hell've you been?" It was a good connection, and Haeflinger's raspy voice came loud and unmistakable across the ocean and parts of continents. "I've been trying to get hold of you all day."

Wilson grunted. He had left the name of the hotel with the hotel desk in Barcelona, knowing Haeflinger got irritated when he couldn't get in touch with his people, so it shouldn't have been that difficult.

"The terrorists've got her," Haeflinger said.

Wilson picked up the tall glass of beer the waiter had set in front of him, and the little cardboard pad with the name of the hotel on it stuck to the bottom of the glass. He knocked it off with his little finger and took a sip.

"What terrorists?" he said.

"How the hell should I know? That's what you gotta find out. I'm here in Chicago."

"Right," Wilson said.

"Listen," Haeflinger said, "we gotta do this right, get it? No fuckups."

"Right," Wilson said. The sound of Haeflinger's voice was beginning to hurt his head.

"You got anything?"

"Nothing much," Wilson said. He ran his hand over the belly that jutted out of the top of his bathing suit. It was about the size and shape of a half watermelon and covered with fine long hairs. Like many bald men, he had plenty of hair on the rest of his body, which didn't seem quite fair.

"That's what I figured," Haeflinger grumbled. "Well, you're gonna have to get your ass in gear."

Wilson took a long swallow of beer and put down the glass. There were small paintings on the wall, watercolors of sailboats, quaint fishermen's cottages, boats drawn up on the sand with their sails down. They looked nice, he thought.

"What's the story?" he said.

"All right, listen. They called up the embassy and said they had her. They said they'd be in touch, they'd issue a statement or something. So the embassy got in touch with Dantry and Dantry called me. And he caught me with my pants down, because you been workin' on this thing for a week and there's nothing in your reports about terrorists. As a matter of fact there's nothing in your reports at all that's worth a shit."

Haeflinger stopped for breath, and Wilson heard him wheezing at the other end of the line.

"Who called the embassy?" he said.

"The terrorists! I told you."

"What terrorists? The ETA?"

"No, not the ETA. They're the ones that blow up cops, aren't they? No, not those guys. Some half-assed terrorists nobody's ever heard of. Nobody but terrorists is gonna be dumb enough to call up the fucking embassy. Those places are full of CIA guys. If those spooks get in on it they'll fuck everything up. That's what you gotta make sure doesn't happen."

Wilson could imagine Haeflinger hunched over his big desk stacked with files, clutching the telephone with one clawlike hand while he picked at the hairs in his nose with the other, his big ugly secretary standing on the other side of the desk glaring down at him. Haeflinger thought she was an excellent secretary, and she had worked for him for years, in spite of the fact that she obviously hated him. Haeflinger liked people hating him, especially his employees. He thought it was the mark of a serious businessman.

"What does Dantry say?"

"He talked to his lawyer," Haeflinger said indignantly, "some hot-shit lawyer he's got in New York—before he talked to me! Well, I talked to Dantry. You leave Dantry to me. I told him that in this kind of thing, the only thing that works is you gotta get in touch with the terrorists and make 'em an offer. Those guys like money, just like everybody else. They need it to buy bombs and stuff like

47

that. The main thing, I told him, is to keep the fucking government out of it, keep politics out of it, because if you don't . . . And keep it out of the papers. He wanted to go out there, supervise things himself. He wants to be a politician, see. He probably figured . . . who knows what he figured . . . maybe he figured it'd be good for his career, heh. I told him. I said, listen, you fuck something like this up, you know, you find your daughter in the woods with a couple of forty-five slugs in her skull. I told him you gotta leave this kind of thing to professionals. I told him we been dealing with scum for forty years."

Haeflinger stopped talking finally and wheezed for a while. Wilson caught the waiter's eye and pointed at his empty glass. "You know my license isn't even valid here?"

"Don't worry about that," Haeflinger said. "Dantry's got clout. I talked to the ambassador and the consul in Barcelona. I told 'em you're representing the Dantry family. The hot-shit lawyer said something about sending somebody over, I figured we had to snuff that fast, heh."

Wilson tried unsuccessfully to imagine Haeflinger talking to an ambassador and took a sip of the beer the waiter set in front of him. "Jesus Christ," he muttered.

"Whatsamatter?" Haeflinger, whose hearing was excellent, demanded. "You don't think you can cut the mustard, I'll get somebody else. The only thing is the only other guy that I got that speaks Spanish is the Puerto Rican and he's in Miami. And I don't really think he can speak Spanish anyway, he talks Puerto Rican."

"Who's got the information?" Wilson said, cutting him off.

"You talk to a guy named Schumacher in the consulate in Barcelona. He's probably a spook. He's got the dope but you'll probably have to suck it out of him. You gotta fuck with 'em, you know. You gotta convince 'em that you're in charge. Understand?"

"Sure," Wilson said, and hung up. Haeflinger wouldn't have sounded that cheerful if he wasn't expecting to make even more money out of this than he had at first. He wondered if Haeflinger had slipped a clause about terrorists into the contract. Haeflinger thought of everything. Maybe he was just figuring on making the Ajax Detective Agency as internationally famous as the Pinkertons. And all Wilson would have to do was make a deal with a terrorist group nobody had ever heard of, keep clear of the CIA and the Spanish cops, and probably a few other things he hadn't thought of yet. And he couldn't expect much help, because Haeflinger, among other things, was a cheapskate.

9

Wilson got back to Barcelona a little after midday. He changed clothes and ate a sandwich in the hotel coffee shop and got to the consulate about three o'clock. There were two policemen with submachine guns dangling from their shoulders in the ground-floor lobby and two more sitting on a wooden table just inside the door of the consulate offices. A fat woman with red hair piled on top of her head sat in a glass booth in front of him with double doors on either side. A tall woman came out the door on the right and said, "They could probably get in anyway, if they wanted to," and the man behind her smiled absentmindedly. They didn't seem very worried about it.

Wilson told the fat woman he wanted to see Mr. Schumacher. She looked at him severely and said, "Passport," through a metal grid in the glass. Wilson took his passport out of the inside pocket of the summer suit he wore when he wanted to impress people and put it in the metal tray in front of her. She looked at the passport, pressed some buttons, and said something he couldn't hear into an intercom. Then she looked at her nail polish.

After a moment she dropped the passport into the tray and

nodded at the door on the left. Wilson pushed it and looked over at her when it didn't open.

"Push!" she shouted, making pushing motions with both hands.

"Push!" one of the policemen said in Spanish, half rising from the table and making similar motions. Wilson pushed the door again, and it opened. He let it close behind him and pushed open the second door and walked into a large, blue-carpeted room with the sun coming in the windows in the far wall.

Wilson stood there for a moment, buttoning and unbuttoning the middle button on his jacket, and then crossed the room and sat down in a chair by the windows. He supposed Schumacher would come out and get him. If he was any kind of a spook he would find him without any trouble.

There were a couple of lines of people with papers in their hands in front of glassed-in windows with numbers above them, and tables where other people were filling out similar papers. A few young men in shorts slouched in comfortable-looking chairs with tanned hairy legs stretched out in front of them, reading old issues of *U.S. News & World Report*, which seemed to be the only magazine around. On the opposite wall there was a medium-size color photograph of the current president and a picture of a very old Indian chief in a war bonnet.

Schumacher was a lean, slightly stooped old man with a long stride. His long white skinny arms came out of a short-sleeved white shirt and he had a big coffee mug in his hand with PRINCETON on it in big letters. Wilson wondered how a guy with a name like Schumacher could ever have got into a snob school like Princeton.

"Mr. Wilson?" Schumacher said. Wilson nodded, standing up, and Schumacher put out a long hand. "Bill Schumacher," he said, peering at him through gold-rimmed glasses. He led Wilson into an alcove off the main room lined with bound volumes of *U.S. News & World Report*, Funk & Wagnall's Encyclopedia yearbooks, a history of the United States in three volumes with little silver stars on the blue binding. They sat down side by side in cushioned chairs with wooden arms. Schumacher sighed and leaned forward over his coffee cup. His hands were white, with long bony fingers, and so dry they crackled when he rubbed them together.

51

"Well," he said.

Wilson took out his pipe, and Schumacher frowned at it.

"I used to smoke a pipe," he said vaguely, still frowning.

"Uh-huh," Wilson said. "We understand they telephoned you."

"Yeah, they did."

"What'd they say?"

Schumacher shook his head. "It's not very clear," he said. He took a sip of his coffee and made a face. It was probably cold, Wilson thought. He was probably always having his coffee get cold in his big fat Princeton cup, and drinking it and making a face.

"They were calling from a pay phone, one of those pay phones that takes your money and then cuts you off. They called a couple of times before they found a phone that worked. They said they had her, and they said they'd call back, but they never did."

"Didn't they identify themselves?"

"Apocalypse," Schumacher said disgustedly. "Said their outfit was called Apocalypse. Nobody's ever heard of them."

"Uh-huh," Wilson said. "And that's all?"

"At the moment, yes," Schumacher said. He had pale-blue watery eyes with fine lines around them. He looked like somebody's grandfather, and probably was.

"You're a veteran, aren't you?"

Wilson grunted. They had checked him out pretty fast, he thought. Schumacher looked into his eyes and pushed out his chin.

"I admire you fellows," he said, "and if you ask me you got a raw deal."

Wilson grunted again. For some reason he thought of Haeflinger in his office with his telephones and his computerized accounting.

"We're looking for you to help us out on this," Schumacher said.

"Sure," Wilson said, "of course."

"You were looking for her before this happened, am I right?"

"That's right."

"What've you come up with?"

"Not much," Wilson said. "She was living with a girlfriend and she moved out, leaving no address, stopped writing her parents. That's about it."

Schumacher nodded. He would know all that, of course.

"It's possible someone will get in touch with you."

"Yeah," Wilson said. That would be nice, he thought. Then all he would have to do would be to haggle the price, make some long-distance phone calls, meet somebody in a dark alley.

"These people," Schumacher said, shaking his head slowly, "you can't make deals with these people. You remember what happened to Aldo Moro?"

Wilson shook his head. The name sounded familiar, but he couldn't place it.

"Italian politician," Schumacher said. "Wanted to make a deal with the Communist Party. Ended up dead in the trunk of a stolen car. Red Brigade shot him. You can't make a deal with the Communists."

Schumacher seemed to think about that for a moment, then his face brightened up a little, as much as it probably ever brightened up. "I saw this show on TV the other night, English program. There was this liberal politician, typical, didn't want any shooting, wanted to negotiate with the crooks, and this tough cop nobody would listen to. In the end the cop was right, of course. They killed the hostages anyway."

Schumacher pursed his lips and nodded with grim satisfaction. "What do you think of Spanish television?"

Wilson shifted his rear on the chair, shrugged and smiled vaguely.

"Course you haven't had a chance to see much of it probably," Schumacher said. "They got a lot of the good programs now, *Falconcrest, Dallas* . . . well, *Dallas* is off now, but . . . It's the Common Market, I suppose. Well, is there anything else you'd like to tell us?"

"I don't think so," Wilson said. He could have mentioned that he had seen *Sesame Street* on afternoon TV, but there didn't seem to be much point.

"Well," Schumacher said. He stood up and shook Wilson's hand. "We'd like to have your cooperation. If they contact you, let us know. Let us know first, before you do anything else. You know what's at stake."

No, Wilson thought, what's at stake? But Schumacher was holding onto his hand as if he weren't going to let it go until he agreed, and Wilson, remembering his grandfather who had had the same kind of parchment-white skin and the same bleary-eyed look of quiet desperation and then had died, nodded idiotically and got out as quickly as he could.

1 0

Wilson stood at the side of the road with the sun on his back, urinating on a cactus. There was a rusted-out car in the gully in front of him and a couple of mountains in the distance left over from a John Ford movie. Wilson had a dry nasty taste in his mouth and a pressure in his head just above and behind the eyes. He zipped up and lumbered back to the car. There were small holes in the dirt, lots of them. If there was a snake to each hole, there would be a lot of snakes, he thought, and decided that wasn't very likely. They probably just liked making holes, probably didn't have much else to do.

She was still sleeping, lying on the backseat with her arm curled over her eyes and her legs tucked up against her body. He stood there for a moment, up against the side of the car, looking at her through the window, not really thinking of anything at all.

It was eight-thirty according to his watch, which meant the sun had been up for a couple of hours, and it was already hot. There were things you had to keep in mind driving on a road like that, especially in the daytime. You had to keep your eye on the gas and oil, and it was a good idea to carry extra water in case you overheated. People died out there sometimes, walking down the road with an empty can to look for water, dropping dead from sunstroke after the first couple hundred yards. He wondered how those people with the wagon trains had managed it. But the people with the wagon trains had probably gone by a different route.

Wilson tried to spit, and what he got out made something like a pinhole in the powdery dirt. He opened the car door, slid behind the wheel, and heard her stir behind him as he put the key in the ignition. The engine coughed for a moment, and Wilson felt a thrill of panic like an electric shock before it caught. Scared, he thought, scared of the desert, scared of being stuck out there, having to mess with some goddammed machine that just stopped working, the way they did sometimes, when they got sick of people pushing them too hard.

He put the car into gear and eased it out onto the highway, taking it gently up through the gears. Tires could go pretty easily on a hot pavement like that, he thought. He couldn't remember ever looking at the tires. The air conditioning still wasn't really working.

Elizabeth leaned forward, resting her arms on the back of the seat in front of her.

"I could use some Coke," she said.

"Sure," Wilson grumbled.

"Coca-Cola, I mean," she said, amused, putting a cigarette in her mouth. "It's good for a hangover. It's the bubbles, I suppose."

"Don't smoke," Wilson said. "It'll dry out your mouth."

"Shit," Elizabeth said, and lit the cigarette. Wilson rubbed his face with one hand and put on his sunglasses. They stared out in silence at the desert opening out in front of them. There were mountains far out ahead, with nothing before them but shimmering waves of heat distortion. Wilson kept on driving.

About half an hour later they saw what was left of a river winding through the dust on the far side of the road. It had dwindled in the summer heat to a narrow stream at the middle of a wide, dried-out riverbed, but there were bushes along the bank, just holding on till the autumn, even a few scraggly trees. The river came closer and then ran alongside the road a few yards from its edge, glittering like metal.

"Why don't we stop for a minute?" Wilson said.

A new-model Chevrolet zipped past pulling a camping trailer with Wisconsin plates, and then the road was empty when Wilson pulled off. Elizabeth got out of the car and walked around behind some bushes. Wilson walked down the slope of the bank to the stream. The dry ground was sprinkled with small smooth stones, and there were more stones at the bottom of the stream. It was shallow and running slow, but the water was clear. Wilson squatted painfully, scooped up some water in both hands and drank, and then slopped water on his face and the back of his neck. She hadn't bothered to take the gun with her. Maybe she had decided to trust him, or maybe she had just forgotten. He squatted there wondering if he could make it to the car and get the gun before she came out of the bushes while he watched the tiny water flies spinning over the surface of the stream. Then she came back and he didn't have to think about it any more.

She knelt down on the stones and plunged her face into the water, and then she raised her head and shook it, sitting back on her heels, grinning, with the water dripping off her nose and her chin. Wilson looked at her maybe a little too long, and she stopped grinning. She stood up and looked off downstream with her hands in her back pockets.

"We better get going," she said after a minute.

There was a town a little way down the river, with a few fields around it cut out of the dry soil with more trouble than they looked like they were worth, and old trees that didn't die out of sheer stubbornness. The International Harvester dealership, in a glass-and-concrete corner building, was the biggest business in town.

Wilson parked in front of the café a few doors down and they went through the flimsy glass-and-aluminum door into air-conditioning and a smell of coffee and fried eggs. It was late for people to be having breakfast in a place like that. Two teenage girls were drinking Cokes and whispering at each other across a linoleum-topped table, and a man who looked like a traveling salesman was picking tiredly through a pile of advertising brochures. Elizabeth ordered a Coke and then they both ate big portions of ham and eggs with hash brown potatoes. When they had finished they smoked and drank more coffee, looking out the big front window, watching the pickup trucks go by.

They would be in Los Angeles that night, Wilson thought. He had the car keys and she had the gun, so it was a kind of standoff for the moment. She didn't seem to mind, didn't seem to notice he was there most of the time, wrapped up in her own thoughts, but he wondered if she would try to get away from him when she got the chance. Maybe not, he thought, maybe she was lonesome.

"What'd you do after you left Munet?" he said.

She looked down at the cigarette between her fingers, smiling faintly, put the plastic ashtray that said BURLEY'S FEED AND GRAIN on it in the center of the table.

"We went to this woods, you know. There were all these people running around in the dark yelling and stuff, and Ramon kept saying this is really great and all, and I thought, This is like cowboys and Indians. I've come three thousand miles to go out and play cowboys and Indians in the dark. So I left. I went back to Barcelona."

"Back to Marjorie's."

"Yeah. Back to Marjorie's."

"And then?"

She sighed and looked out the big window. "I don't think I want to talk about that," she said softly. "Not right now."

11

Marjorie Walters was standing in the doorway of the apartment when Wilson got off the elevator. She was wearing a flowery print skirt and a loose green T-shirt, and didn't look any happier than the last time he had seen her.

Wilson walked past her into the living room and sat down on the sofa. The sun was still shifting genteelly through the leaves outside the window. He took out his pipe and started filling it, taking his time. "Cops been to see you?"

She said "Yes," and sat down at the work table in front of the windows. There were books and magazines in neat stacks on the table, and pencils lined up side by side. She rested an elbow on it.

"I don't mind people lying to me," Wilson said slowly. "I'm kind of used to it. But I suppose you told the cops the truth, didn't you?"

"Elizabeth told me . . . not to tell anyone."

"Uh-huh," Wilson said, putting a match to his pipe. "Not to tell anyone what?"

"I don't know where she is," Marjorie said with a little tremor in her voice.

"Yeah," Wilson said. "You said that before. You still think nothing's going to happen to her?"

She looked at him miserably and straightened her skirt.

"Just tell me what you told the cops first," he suggested. "Then you can tell me the rest."

He lit his pipe again and puffed on it, letting her get a little more uncomfortable. "Where'd she go when she moved out of here?"

"I told you. I don't know."

"Did she move in with some guy maybe?"

Marjorie kept her eyes on the floor, seemed to shake her head, and then said, in a little voice, "Maybe she did."

"What's his name?"

"Juan."

"Last name?"

"I don't know."

Wilson took a couple of puffs on his pipe, and she looked distractedly at the smoke, wrinkling her nose. "But you knew him, right?"

"I only met him a couple of times."

"Okay. What's he look like?"

"He's sort of medium, kind of thin. He's got brown hair, sort of reddish brown. He seemed nice." She waved her rather stubby fingers in the air and fell silent.

"What does he do?"

"I don't know."

Wilson sighed and sat up a little straighter. "You're not much help, you know that, Miss Walters?"

She stared at him with a kind of blank, prim stubbornness on her red face. Wilson was used to people disliking him, it didn't particularly bother him. There was something pathetic about her, but it irritated him more than made him feel sorry for her.

"There's something I don't quite understand," he said. "You don't seem to like her too much, she didn't do the dishes and she walked out on you, but you're willing to tell quite a lot of lies just because she asked you to. That doesn't quite make sense to me."

She wrinkled her forehead and her eyes got bigger, then she

looked over with a sudden interest at a big potted plant in the corner of the room.

"Was she getting it on with you too?" Wilson watched her face go even redder, the features collapse as if she were about to start crying, and went on in the same even tone, "I mean, she seems to have been making it with quite a few people . . . Or maybe you just wanted to?"

"I don't see why I have to talk to you," she said when she got her breath.

"Yes, you do," Wilson said quickly. He had the feeling he could smell his sweat, stale and nasty like the smell in the subway car he had taken that morning.

"Come on," he said. "You like getting pushed around. Elizabeth pushed you around, didn't she? Took over your place and made a mess of it. Did the cops push you around a little?"

"They were polite!" she said hoarsely. "One of them spoke English."

"Old World charm," Wilson sneered, and then more gently, "I just want a little information, Miss Walters. Like why Elizabeth moved out just a few weeks before she was kidnapped. You understand? And I guess you know the answer."

She glared at him, opened her mouth but nothing came out.

"What do you think? That your friend the cop that speaks English is gonna find her?"

A light breeze came through the window and rattled the bullfight poster on the wall.

"She started talking about politics all the time," Marjorie said, looking at the floor, with a whine in her voice. "She said America was guilty, we were all guilty. Of the people starving in Africa, torture and wars. She was nasty about it. Like it was my fault."

"Uh-huh," Wilson said quietly. "Did you tell the cops that?"

"No."

"That's good," Wilson said, though he wasn't sure why. "Did you see her at all after she moved out?"

"Once. She left a bunch of stuff here. She had a lot of stuff. I told her she couldn't just leave it here."

"She didn't tell you what she was doing, anything about where she was living?"

61

"She was cutting me off. That's what she's like. She's a cold person basically."

Her voice was under control again, flat and uninterested. Wilson knocked out his pipe into a ceramic ashtray. "Did the cops show you any photos?"

"Yes, but Juanjo wasn't in any of them."

"Juanjo?"

"Elizabeth always called him Juanjo," she said dully.

"That's Juan José, isn't it?"

Marjorie didn't bother to answer. She put her elbows on her knees and rested her chin on her hands.

"You remember anything special about him at all?"

"He's got a kind of hole in his chin, here," she said, putting a fingertip on the center of her chin. "Like Kirk Douglas, you know?"

Wilson nodded, put the pipe in his pocket, and stood up. "Thanks," he said, and realized he was grinning. She looked up at him with an expression of dull hatred and watched him walk to the door.

"I did it because she's my friend," she said behind him. "You wouldn't understand that."

Wilson spat into the flower bed in front of the building and stood there for a moment scraping out the bowl of his pipe with a short knife. There weren't many people on the street, a woman walking a silver poodle that matched her hair, a lanky kid with a math book under his arm scuffing the shine on his ox-blood loafers. On the other side of the street a young man with earphones on was sitting behind the steering wheel of a yellow Renault tapping the dashboard to the music and trying to look like he was waiting for somebody. Wilson took a good look at him, in case he ran into him again.

Wilson smoked a joint while he watched the late-night movie, and then sat up, since he was expecting Haeflinger to call, reading *The Pickwick Papers*. Mr. Pickwick fell through the ice on a skating pond, his friends fished him out and took him home in a barrow, and they sat around the fire drinking hot brandy. It was old-fashioned but Wilson was enjoying it. He liked to take long books with him when he was traveling, classics that he could count on and would not finish in one night, because he didn't like finding himself with nothing to read in a strange town. Haeflinger finally called a little after two o'clock.

"What'd that Schumacher guy say?" he shouted.

"He asked me what I thought of Spanish television."

"They're shifty bastards," Haeflinger said, "I told you." His voice sounded charged with overwrought enthusiasm. He had probably had three or four bourbons by then, Wilson thought, calculating the time over there. He was in bed, his book propped on his chest and a warm pipe in his hand. He turned a page.

"You gotta get ahold of those terrorists," Haeflinger growled, "let 'em know they gotta talk to us, not the goddam consulate."

"How do you suggest I do that?" Wilson said tiredly.

"How the hell should I know?" Haeflinger exploded. "I'm over here in Chicago."

"Maybe put something in the personals?" Wilson said. He was getting sick of Haeflinger, he had been getting sick of him ever since he started working for the Ajax Detective Agency.

"Wilson," Haeflinger said, "you think terrorists read the personals?"

"I don't know. I never thought about it."

"I'm working this thing over here," Haeflinger said, ignoring him. "Dantry's breathing down my neck . . ."

"How much is he ready to put out?" Wilson interrupted.

"What d'you mean?" Haeflinger snapped. He didn't like talking about money with his employees.

"I mean, how much is he willing to pay?"

"We don't even know how much they want," Haeflinger sputtered. "He's got money. We'll worry about that when we come to it. Right now you get your ass in gear. And get me a decent report. I gotta give the son of a bitch something."

"What I mean to say," Wilson said, "is that I'm gonna need money to work with. If I want people to talk to me. You understand?"

"Yeah," Haeflinger growled. "Itemize it."

"How much can I offer? For hard information?"

Haeflinger breathed for a while, uneven and panicky across the international wires. "Five hundred maybe."

"Shit," Wilson said.

"That's a lot of money over there!"

"Not anymore. The dollar's gone down, haven't you heard?"

"All right. A thousand if it's really good. And I want a telex tomorrow. With something in it that's worth a shit."

"Sure," Wilson said. They would find her eventually, on a slab in the morgue or smiling bravely for the cameras because she had always known her daddy would pay for somebody to get her out of this, and after all it was one way to get your face in the papers. He told Haeflinger not to worry.

"Yeah," Haeflinger said. "I got work to do."

Wilson finished the chapter and turned out the light.

12

It was in the newspapers the next day, "North American Student Kidnapped by Apocalypse Terrorists" or something to that effect, short, choppy articles that sounded as if they were not quite sure they believed it. Wilson telephoned the most intelligent-looking newspaper and left a message for the reporter covering the story to call him. A little while after lunch a guy named Emili Valcarca phoned, and they agreed to meet at a café in an hour.

Wilson got there first, with a *Time* magazine under his arm that Valcarca had asked him to carry so he could recognize him. The day was hot and almost windless, with a faint, suspicious-looking haze in the air and a mild, persistent stink of indeterminable origin. The café was in a square that was closed to automobile traffic, paved with gray cement blocks and bounded all around by old apartment buildings with curly iron balustrades and rubbery-looking plants on the balconies. There was a sprinkling of dirty gray pigeons that fluttered wearily up into the tops of skinny trees when one of the numerous dogs decided to charge them. Small children chased one another noisily across the pavement and older ones sat drinking beer from liter bottles and listening to Michael Jackson on a big cassette

65

player. Wilson sat down at one of the white metal tables in front of the café, put the magazine on the tabletop, and ordered a beer. Then he sat there, with the round face of Adnan Khasoggi, the world's smoothest arms trader, smiling up at him from the cover. The sun on his belly made him pleasantly sleepy.

Emili Valcarca wasn't difficult to spot, loping across the square toward the café with a look of hurried determination and a cloth bag hanging from his shoulder. He was tall and skinny, with a long neck and a small round head that made him look a little like an insect, short hair and a small black beard, brown eyes bright and slightly bloodshot behind horn-rimmed glasses. He looked young, overserious, overeager, and probably overworked.

They shook hands and Valcarca slumped into a metal chair, dropping his shoulder bag onto the pavement beside him. He asked Wilson more or less obvious questions and wrote things down in a little notebook. Wilson told him most of what he knew, which didn't sound like much.

"So you're a private detective?" Valcarca said. Wilson wondered if he was being ironic, and then when he said, "Is that why you smoke a pipe?" he decided he was just a silly ass.

"I used to smoke cigarettes," Wilson said, nodding at Valcarca's pack of Marlboros, "but I started coughing up globs of yellow stuff in the morning. Your paper says they telephoned you."

"Not us. *La Vanguardia*. That's another paper."

"What did they say?"

"They said they had the girl, said they were against disinformation and the manipulation of the media. Nobody printed that, of course."

Wilson wondered if he was being ironic again. Wilson's Spanish was good, but not always good enough to catch all the nuances, and Valcarca had a monotonous, clipped way of talking that didn't really fit with his studious look. Perhaps he had copied it from some tough reporter on television or from some veteran around the press room whom he filled in for on shit jobs like this one.

"Of course?"

"There's a kind of unwritten law. There are a lot of groups that want to call attention to themselves. Planting a bomb someplace or hijacking an airplane is a pretty good way to get into the papers, but we don't print their press releases."

"So what's this Apocalypse group?"

Valcarca shook his head. "Nobody knows. The police are checking the statement."

"For what?"

"They analyze the wording, the terminology, compare it by computer with documents from terrorist organizations in Europe and the Near East. The idea is that every ideology, every group, has its own jargon. They cross-check for influences, connections."

"And what do they think?"

"They're keeping very quiet about it so far. Our guess is that they don't know. They don't know how big this is, and that makes them nervous. Have they talked to you yet?"

"No," Wilson said uneasily. He didn't want to talk to any nervous cops. He ate an olive and tossed the pit out onto the pavement. A pigeon pecked at it speculatively and then swallowed it with a gulp.

"What do you figure are the possibilities?"

"The possibilities," Valcarca repeated thoughtfully. He was young enough to get a kick out of being asked for his analysis of the situation, even if he didn't want to show it. He probably didn't know a hell of a lot, Wilson thought, but more than Wilson did, anyway.

"You can rule out the known organizations—or a split from one of them. There's nobody that operates at all like this. Could be common criminals using a political cover. But calling the consulate, that sounds like amateurs. And amateurs," he said solemnly, "can be dangerous."

Wilson suppressed a snicker and said, "Go on."

Valcarca drank some beer and lowered his voice a little. "Rumor has it the indications point toward an anarchist operation. If it is, it's not likely to last long."

"Why's that?"

"In the first years of the democratic transition," Valcarca said, "anarchist groups were infiltrated up, down, and sideways. Martin Villa. Minister of the interior Martin Villa. Nasty character, but efficient. That was around the time of the Baader Meinhof, remember. He got help from the German police, he bought a German computer. Police spies, *agents provocateurs*, it's an interesting, untold story. Somebody ought to do it up some day."

"When did all this happen?"

"Ten years ago now, more or less."

"I don't quite see how that makes it so easy."

"The activists are all on file. Anyone who's involved in this is going to be on file somewhere. They'll just sort of swoop them up."

"Uh-huh," Wilson said. A hungry-looking terrier nuzzled Valcarca's bag and he shooed it away, making fluttery, nervous motions with his hands.

"What do you suppose they want?"

Valcarca shrugged. "Who knows? Anarchists are . . . unpredictable." He seemed to find that funny for some reason.

"But this is just a rumor, understand. The police don't want to put their foot in it. On the other hand they've been caught by surprise, they're supposed to see this kind of thing coming. So they're under pressure to come up with something quick."

He leaned back, nodding. The terrier rubbed its cold nose on Wilson's bare ankle. Wilson jumped and Valcarca threw him a puzzled frown before he went on.

"We're keeping the pressure on. I expect to have something from them by tonight."

Wilson asked him to let him know when he heard something, wrote the hotel phone number on a business card and gave it to him. Valcarca frowned at the card for a moment, as if wondering what, if anything, he was getting in return, then nodded and trotted off across the square, dodging dogs and small children on tricycles.

Wilson ordered another beer and wrote a few things in his own little notebook. He didn't know much about anarchists, aside from what he had read once in a book about Sacco and Vanzetti, and that wouldn't help much, since as far as he could remember the point of the story was that Sacco and Vanzetti hadn't done it.

He took the list Munet had given him of the participants in the theatrical experimental workshop in the woods out of his pocket and laid it flat on the table. There were three Juans, but no Juan Josés, not even any Juan Jorges or Juan Horacios. It didn't seem like an especially good angle, but he really didn't have anything else to do. He looked up the addresses in the street guide he had bought a couple of days before, and picked a Juan Altarés Malagueño who lived in the city center for his first stop. It wasn't far, so he walked, looking at the shop windows and women's legs.

The address was in one of those narrow streets that the sun only hits a couple hours of the year, solitary and picturesque and ideal for muggings. The place was up three flights of irregular stairs, and there was an eviction notice on the door when he got to it, dated two months before. The fat lady on the other side of the landing said she hadn't seen Altarés for longer than that, though she wasn't quite sure which one he was anyway.

At the next place a woman in a bathrobe answered the door and stood twisting a plait of thick dark hair around her hand while she looked him over. Juan wasn't there, she said, he had gone to Avignon for the festival. Wilson said he was talking to people who had known Elizabeth Dantry on Munet's workshop.

"Yeah," she said lazily. "I saw Elizabeth's picture on television." She cocked a hip and squinted at him. "Are you some kind of police?"

"Private investigator," Wilson mumbled. "You know her?"

"I was on that thing of Munet's too," she said. She was tall, and in spite of the bulky terry-cloth bathrobe he could guess she had a statuesque, Greek goddess sort of figure. Her brown eyes were large and sleepy looking. "Sorry," she said. "I'm still kind of dopey. I was flaked out."

She led him into a small living room with a low sofa in front of the television. A police car squealed around a corner in what looked like an American television series, a woman screamed and dropped her groceries. Juan's friend stood staring vaguely down at the screen, maybe trying to catch up on what she had missed. There was a lingering smell of pork chops and garlic.

"You want some coffee?" she said when the commercials started. "I'm making some coffee."

"Thanks," Wilson said. From where he stood the kitchen looked about three feet across and stacked with pots and pans. He sat down on the sofa and watched a diaper ad in which a lineup of naked babies obviously too young to talk enthusiastically admitted that they pissed a lot. She brought out two little cups of coffee and handed him a sugar bowl, then sat down beside him on the sofa, watching the television while she drank her coffee.

"I didn't really get to know her very well," she said, pulling the skirts of her bathrobe over her knees and then letting them slip off again. "The English, I mean the Americans, they're like the English, you know, reserved. You never know what they're thinking. Maybe they aren't thinking anything."

She giggled, and leaned forward to drink more coffee, and Wilson looked cautiously down the front of her bathrobe.

"But she was nice. She didn't really know what was going on, poor thing, and she was sort of following Munet around all the time, so some people didn't like her, but I thought she was nice. Because Munet—well, Munet's a jerk, isn't he? I mean, there was this story that we were going to form a troupe, he was going to get us a grant from the Ministry of Culture and all that. That's why most people went, really, and what it was, it was this experiment he was doing for his doctoral thesis, see. We were like these little guinea pigs in his laboratory—that's what everybody says now—and we even had to pay for it."

She shrugged and looked at the TV again. A blonde in a baseball cap was holding a chimpanzee in her arms and talking to a gray-haired uniformed policeman.

"Well, it was interesting anyway, I guess. Different."

"You know if she got involved with anybody there besides Munet?"

"Involved?" she said, grinning, and shook her head. "I don't think anybody got involved there. They just screwed a lot, you know? Sometimes it just seemed like there were a lot of bodies around."

"Uh-huh," Wilson said uneasily, looking at her knees.

"She really has been kidnapped?"

"Apparently."

"That's really weird," she said.

Wilson took the subway out to the last address. Coming up the stairs to the street he saw a blue-gray cloud of exhaust fumes hanging over endless lines of cars, great blocks of apartment buildings, one after another and almost identical except for the colors. They looked as if they had been thrown up ten, twenty, or thirty years ago, all at about the same time and as quickly as possible, like a colony on Mars. He found the address and went up in an elevator that clunked at each floor. A small young woman with dirty blond hair opened the door and looked at him as if she expected bad news. She was wearing a short skirt and a green halter top, and her small breasts made little points in the material. He asked for Juan Jilguero, and she said he wasn't there.

"Do you know where I could find him?"

"What is it?" she said. She reminded him of those feisty little dogs that try to bite people's ankles to make up for having been born small. He was trying his nice-guy smile, but he could see she wasn't buying it.

"I just want to talk to him. It's about a friend of his."

"Who are you?"

Wilson sighed. "Private investigator," he said, handing her one of his cards.

She looked at it and wrinkled her nose. "It's in English."

"I know," Wilson said. "I just want some information."

"Maybe he's at the studio," she said dubiously.

"Where's that?"

"It's hard to find."

"I'll make an effort," Wilson said.

You walked down to the end of a side street and across a field of dusty weeds, dotted with piles of garbage, to a place where it looked as if somebody had started to build a supermarket and then changed his mind. The studio was in a kind of hut built up against the red brick wall of a long-abandoned factory building.

There was a path worn up to the door through the weeds, and a confusion of clanging and banging noises—like a metalworker's shop going full tilt—could be heard from quite a distance away. The door was made of worm-eaten planks and slabs of plywood held together with metal strips and covered with signs that read DANGER, FALLOUT AREA, HIGH VOLTAGE, KEEP OUT, RESTRICTED AREA, NO ENTRY WITHOUT SAFETY HELMET. Wilson knocked a couple of times, and when no one answered he went in.

Inside the noise was infernal. The dirt floor was greasy black, crisscrossed with cables and littered with apparatus and chunks of old machines. There were four men with earphones, three of them

71

bent over complicated-looking electronic gadgets spread out in a tangle of wires over a wooden sawhorse table, while the fourth beat a piece of sheet metal with a wooden hammer at irregular intervals. The sound of a metal saw was coming from somewhere, loud and grating, growing steadily more shrill until it approximated something like a human scream.

Eventually one of them noticed Wilson and began yelling at him incomprehensibly until somebody cut the sound.

"You see the sign on the door, Charlie? Who asked you in?"

They looked young and fairly outlandish, in baggy trousers or worn jeans and dirty T-shirts, their faces liberally smeared with sweat and grease. It was terrifically hot in the shack, a stifling, dirty heat, and the four of them, all shouting and gesticulating at him at once, seemed sort of comically menacing, as if they were really quite enjoying themselves.

"Juan Jilguero," Wilson shouted. "I'm looking for Juan Jilguero."

The guy with the wooden hammer said, "That's me," put down the hammer, and walked over to where Wilson was standing. His head had been shaved, and the hair had been growing out for a few days, probably about the same length of time that he had neglected to shave, so that there was a uniform dark stubble over most of his head and face.

"It's about Elizabeth Dantry," Wilson said. "You know her, right?"

Jilguero shrugged, wrinkling his forehead. "If I know her? Yeah, well, I sort of know her, I guess. What do you want?"

"I'd like to talk to you for a minute," Wilson said, nodding at the door.

Jilguero shrugged again, said something to the others, and they stepped outside. In the field the smell of pale-green weeds blended curiously with the smell of burned gasoline on the air.

"So what's happening?" Jilguero said.

"Elizabeth's disappeared," Wilson said. "I'm looking for information."

Jilguero looked at him quizzically for a moment, rubbing the side of his nose with a dirty forefinger. "You want a beer?"

Wilson nodded, and they took the path back across the field.

72

A group of kids on the other side were throwing rocks at empty cognac bottles.

"Who are you?" Jilguero said.

"Name's Wilson. I'm working for Elizabeth's parents."

The sound of the metal saw came out of the hut again, mixed with clanging sounds, distorted sirens, all out of time. No rhythm, Wilson thought, or maybe some kind of rhythm he couldn't hear.

"You a private detective?" Jilguero said, smiling satirically.

Wilson nodded.

"That a good job?"

"You get to travel," Wilson said. "You're a musician?"

"No," Jilguero said scornfully, and jerked a thumb over his shoulder. "You think that's music? No. That's noise, man, noise. Antimusic, maybe. Music's dead. Like words. Any music you make, in a couple of years you'll be listening to it in an elevator."

They turned into a side street and went through the open door of a small, dusty-looking bar. The television in the corner was turned up loud on an old American science-fiction series in which humanity was being infiltrated by lizard creatures from another galaxy. Jilguero told the woman behind the bar to bring them two beers, and they sat down at a table with a sticky vinyl top.

"It's all background music, see? Rock 'n' roll?" Jilguero linked his fingers and made a cradling motion. "Rock people to sleep. That's the idea. We don't wanta put people to sleep. We wanta wake 'em up."

The woman put the beers on the table, and Jilguero drank some from the bottle and asked for a bag of potato chips. A boy about three or four years old was riding a tricycle with plastic wheels around the tables.

"But you got people doing stuff like this in America, don't you?"

"I don't know," Wilson said.

"Sure. I heard some tapes."

"You went on this thing with Munet, didn't you?"

"Yeah," Jilguero said, leaning back, caressing the fuzz on the top of his head. "Yeah. That was, ah . . . I learned a lot there, yeah. I mean, Munet, Munet's smart, you know. He knows how to get things to happen, and then, it's funny, he got it all to happen and

73

then he, he didn't really know what was going on. Because basically he's an asshole, see."

He drank some more beer and paused, considering. "Music isn't really the problem, it's not the music, it's the people. They can't hear. Silence would be better, maybe, okay, but there isn't any silence. It's impossible. The air's full of noise. So we make more noise. We make so much noise it's like silence. See?"

He rubbed his stomach, tore open the bag of potato chips with his teeth, and stuffed a handful into his mouth.

"Can you make money on that?" Wilson said.

"No," Jilguero said contemptuously. "If we were in Madrid . . . If we were in Madrid we'd probably have a grant, because we're doing shit nobody else is doing."

"You mean a grant from the government?"

"Yeah." Jilguero laughed. "They wanta buy out the opposition, see, and the opposition is us. And we're hungry. But Barcelona's fucked. Barcelona's got real backward."

He shook his head. "I don't know. It's like Molière, you know. He was in the right place and he met the right people, so he got to be Molière. You know what I mean?"

Wilson poured himself some more beer. "Did you know Elizabeth very well?"

"No," Jilguero said, glancing over at the TV, scooping up some more potato chips, "not really. What's the story?"

Wilson took out his pipe and started filling it, crushing the tobacco between his fingers.

"Apparently she's been kidnapped," he said, "by some sort of terrorist group."

Jilguero swallowed some beer and made a face. "What's that mean? It's just a word. I don't believe in words. Especially that kind of word."

"Well," Wilson said mildly, "somebody kidnapped her."

Jilguero scratched behind his ear and said, "Yeah."

"There was a lot of action at this thing of Munet's?"

Jilguero shrugged, digging into the bag for the last of the potato chips. Wilson lit his pipe and puffed on it for minute.

"Did you make it with her?" he said between puffs.

"Yeah," Jilguero said with a grin, "yeah, I did. I like to screw.

I'm not obsessed or anything, I just like it. There was a lot of fucking going on there. There wasn't anything . . ."

"Anything personal about it," Wilson suggested.

"Exactly."

"Do you remember anyone else she was, uh, friends with?"

"No. Nobody paid any attention to who was making it with who."

"Have you seen her since?"

"No. I wouldn't mind seeing her, but . . . no." Jilguero finished his beer and bounced the bottom of the bottle on the table.

"You in a hurry?" Wilson said.

"No."

"I understand she left before the end of . . . before it ended. Do you have any idea why?"

"No," Jilguero said, leaning on the table. "Look, it wasn't like . . . You didn't get to know people, because everybody was . . . we were making movies all the time. Everybody was making his own movie. I cleared up some ideas there. The woods, you know, it was the woods mostly. Maybe that's why I'm here now. But I didn't pay much attention to the people. I been around people all my life, right? I paid attention to the woods."

"What do you do for a living, Juan?"

Jilguero glanced at him quickly, chuckled. "I'm a mechanic, motorcycle mechanic. When I'm working."

Wilson nodded. "You know of anybody that might have seen her since then?"

"No."

"No idea?"

Jilguero shook his head. Wilson looked at his face for a moment, then pushed back his chair.

"I've gotta get going," he said. He paid for the beers and gave Jilguero a card with the hotel phone number on it. They separated at the corner, and Jilguero told him how to get to the subway.

13

Wilson bought a plastic five-gallon container for water at the hardware store and a six-pack of beer and some matches at the grocer's. She was leaning against the car when he came back, and gave him a small humorous smile when she saw the six-pack.

"I get thirsty when I drive," he said.

"I can drive, you know."

"Sure, but I'm getting paid for this," Wilson said, and then wished he hadn't.

They bought gas at the filling station, had the oil checked, and filled the plastic container with water. Then they drove out past the old western-style hotel with second-story porches and different colors of paint peeling off the boards and the California-style bungalows and the irrigation ditches and onto the highway that curved gently up toward yellow, rough-hewn mountains. Wilson cracked open a beer, drank, and set the can in his crotch, feeling the cold moist metal through his trousers. After a while he leaned over and opened the glove compartment in front of her and took out a crushed cigarette pack. He shook a joint out of it and put the pack back in the glove compartment, snapped it shut, and held the joint out to her.

She looked at it and said, "What's that, truth serum?"

"If you don't want any, just gimme the lighter," Wilson said, putting his hand on the wheel.

"I don't know." She gave him the lighter and twisted a beer out of the six-pack. She looked out the side window at the yellow rock that had tumbled down the side of the mountain a few thousand years before. "I don't want to go through anything."

"Yeah," Wilson said vaguely. He hadn't been thinking about that, he hadn't been thinking about anything really, as far as he knew. The road and the heat had steamed his brains, but there wasn't anything to think about anyway. It was just a matter of going through the motions. Because it was all already decided, set, and he was the automatic pilot. He had the joint between his fingers so he lit it, took the smoke into his lungs and held it there, and passed her the joint without looking. He felt her fingers brush his as she took it.

The ground rose so gradually there that you sometimes hardly noticed that you were climbing. You came slowly up out of the desert, and when you finally hit the mountains you were a long time in among them before you came out again. They were hard and craggy, what the geologists called young mountains that hadn't had time to turn soft. You looked at them, and you didn't think there could be much of anything living out there, but there was.

"One time," Wilson said, "one time I was up in the Rockies in Colorado, and I was, I was pretty stoned, and I was climbing around with this friend of mine. We climbed up to this peak, well, it wasn't really a peak, it was just this place that was pretty high. It was a rough climb, scrambling, and we got up to the top and started walking, and we came to this place, it was like tree trunks, not very tall, like columns, no branches, on this flat space of ground, I mean, really flat, like a floor. And they were all stone, the tree trunks, I mean, kind of pale green and white, milky white, like marble kind of, and the ground was the same, stone, I mean, and the same color. It was pretty weird. And then we walked on a little ways and we saw this eagle, gliding around in the sky. At least we thought it was an eagle. We were pretty stoned."

"A petrified forest," Elizabeth said. "There was a movie called *The Petrified Forest*. With Humphrey Bogart."

Wilson drew on the end of the joint and held it out to her. There wasn't much left of it. "You want the rest of this?"

She shook her head, and Wilson stubbed it out in the ashtray. There were trees along the side of the road then, scrub pines and fir trees, climbing up and down the ravines with their deep electric-green branches.

"Yeah. I never saw it," Wilson said.

"I saw it in Barcelona," Elizabeth said, "on television." That struck her as funny somehow. She giggled and drank some beer from the can.

"Shit," she said. "I've got the shakes."

She said it flatly, like a clinical observation. Wilson let up a little on the gas and glanced at her. She didn't seem to look any different.

"You know, all this," she said, waving vaguely at the window, "it's just like television. The scenery, I mean. Like they run it by your window and you think you're going someplace. I bet if we got out it'd just be some suburb somewhere."

She giggled again and then stared out with a slightly confused skeptical stare, sitting up straight while the rocks and the tall green trees went by.

"Fucking petrified forest," she said. "My dad took me to see a petrified forest once. You can pay five bucks for your mystical experience."

"Gimme another beer, would you?" Wilson said.

When she handed him the beer he thought he saw the tension around her mouth and eyes, he could hear it in any case in her voice. He hoped she wouldn't start crying or screaming. He had no idea what he would do about it if she did.

"Just take it easy," he said. "Marijuana wears off pretty quick. Drink your beer."

She put on some sunglasses and stuck a cigarette in her mouth. Her hands didn't seem to shake when she lit it; he wondered if that meant anything.

"I suppose you were in Vietnam, weren't you?" she said.

"Yeah," Wilson said stiffly, glancing at the dark lenses on her glasses. "What? Does it show?"

"You're the right age, you're almost a cop. So I'm sitting in

78

this car with this Vietnam veteran. I hear they go berserk sometimes, just right out of the blue."

"That isn't very funny," Wilson said quietly.

"There was this veteran in Boulder. He had a hollow leg, plastic, I guess he had some kind of disability pension because he didn't do anything, he just hung around. He wasn't from around there, he was from Pennsylvania or someplace like that, I think. He lived in this shack and guys from my high school used to go up there sometimes with a case of beer and get him to tell them 'gook stories.' That's what they called them, 'gook stories.' That's the kind of people I went to high school with.

"He got to be kind of a town joke after a while. He was supposed to be some kind of hero, see? And I guess he really was, because he had these medals, but after a while he sort of ran out of stories. And then he started making them up. His imagination wasn't that great, I guess, he wasn't that sharp in general. He was hanging around with these high school kids all the time, he didn't realize they were just putting him on. Well, I guess he did realize eventually. He shot a kid, and they took him off to the Veteran's Hospital."

She looked over at Wilson with a crooked smile under her dark glasses, but he was keeping his eyes on the road. She switched on the radio and found a country-western station. A guy with a deep voice was singing about how his wife drove away with another man and how they went off a slippery curve down the road a ways. Wilson opened up another beer.

They came down out of the mountains, and a little after noon they reached Phoenix, a white, low-slung town sprawled out over an arid plain, all concrete and glass and plastic signs. They ate chili con carne and drank more coffee at a truck stop café with a view of a stretch of highway shining greasy black in the sun and a Safeway supermarket. Wilson bought another six-pack and kept on driving. He had the feeling he could drive all the way, if nothing went wrong and he was kept supplied with beer. They might not make it by nightfall, but they would make it some time that night. If nothing went wrong.

He saw the yellow bubble on the top of the state trooper's car when it was still a good distance away, coming toward them through the heat haze rising off the pavement.

"Get that beer under the seat," he said, letting up a little on the gas.

"What's the matter," Elizabeth said, "are you underage?" But she got the beer under the seat.

The patrol car slid by and kept on going. Wilson felt the trooper's eyes glance over him without much interest, and that was it.

So they weren't onto his car yet, or at least they hadn't broadcast it, Wilson thought, relieved, and wondered what that meant. He gulped some beer from the can and shook his head. He knew he wasn't thinking too clearly, he probably hadn't been thinking too clearly for quite awhile. Because there wasn't really anything to think about. He didn't have to call Haeflinger. The only thing he had to do was wait for the goddammed FBI men to catch up to them and try to make sure she didn't shoot any of them. That was all.

They had driven north from the motel for a while, but there were still only two places where they could cross the Colorado River into California coming from the southeast. And Wilson seemed to remember that they stopped you sometimes at the border coming in from Arizona. To check for plants or fruit, he thought it was, though they might take the opportunity to see if you had any illegal Mexicans or dope or anything interesting like that. The men could just sit on the border and wait for him and the girl. So there wasn't that much time after all.

"So tell me about Juanjo," Wilson said casually.

She raised her eyebrows, even seemed to smile faintly. She was keeping up with him, beer for beer, but she didn't look loaded, a little blurry perhaps, but everything looked blurry then in that sun—or suddenly, painfully sharp.

"What for?" she said.

"I've been working on this for quite a while. You get curious, you know?"

She shrugged. The desert kept on slipping past the windows, unchanging. Time was different there, stretched out and empty. Most things didn't seem to make much difference.

"What do you wanta know?"

"How did you meet him?"

"I was at this bar with some people, and he was there, with some people in the group—I don't know what he was doing in a place like that—looking kind of miserable. I asked him what was the matter and he said he didn't like Americans. Just like that. There was just me and another American girl, all the other people were Spanish, but . . . Anyway, I'd had a couple of gin and tonics and I was feeling kind of frisky, you know, so I asked him if he wanted to dance. He said he didn't know how, and I said, 'That's okay, I don't either.' So we danced. It was true, he really didn't know how to dance. And then we started talking. He told me all about how he didn't like Americans."

"What'd he say?"

She pushed back her hair and looked out the side window.

"I don't think I feel like talking about politics just now," she said finally.

Wilson started to say something, but she was already going on.

"I was on the wrong side," she said, looking at the dust, "when I didn't even know I was on any side at all. It's funny, you go to college, get your degree, and the one thing they forget to tell you is that you're on the wrong side."

She brushed the hair off her forehead again, looked at the pile of crushed cigarette butts in the ashtray. "And he was right, you know. Juanjo was almost always right. Not that it made any difference."

14

There were two cops waiting for him in the lobby when he got back to the hotel, sitting on a deep couch opposite the desk leafing through magazines with girls in lacy underwear on the covers. They wore casual clothes, light summer jackets to cover up their shoulder holsters. One was blond and looked like a promising young soccer player, the dark one looked like a small-time gangster, but mostly they looked like cops.

The desk clerk said, "These gentlemen have been waiting to see you," not very happy about it, letting him know that it wasn't the kind of hotel that liked having cops sitting around in the lobby. The cops had already put down their magazines and stood up. They didn't look particularly threatening, but that, Wilson thought, didn't mean anything.

They asked him if he was Wilson and he said he was. They showed him some badges, and the blond one said his boss wanted to see him.

"Yeah," Wilson said, waited a second, and then said, "You mean now?"

"We've got a car in front," the cop said.

The car was parked up on the sidewalk with a parking ticket under the windshield wiper. The dark cop pulled it out, got in behind the wheel, and stuffed the ticket down under the dashboard. The blond cop offered Wilson the front seat and got in the back.

The long hot summer afternoon was dragging on to an end, and the traffic was snarled under a bilious cloud. The sidewalks were crowded, and on the wide pavement in front of a fortress like department store there were peddlers with folding tables selling a variety of cheap jewelry and plastic toys. One of them was demonstrating a bubble pipe and the air was full of soap bubbles bursting in the sheer yellow sunlight.

The dark cop offered Wilson a Winston, holding onto the steering wheel with one hand, and said, "What part of America are you from?"

"No thanks," Wilson said, "Chicago."

"Chicago, huh," the cop said, nodding. "Lot of gangsters in Chicago, eh?"

"Fair amount," Wilson said. "How are you doing for gangsters?"

The cop glanced over at him and broke into a hacking laugh. The cop in the backseat laughed too, but made a little less noise.

"We're doing all right," the dark one said, looking back at the other for confirmation. "It's not Chicago, but we're getting there."

He drove up onto the sidewalk in front of a place with leaded windows and a small copper plaque that read SCOTCH CLUB beside the door. Inside there was air-conditioning, dark wood, and pewter beer mugs dangling from hooks over the bar. There didn't seem to be anybody there but a bartender in a black suit. They walked Wilson back to a padded booth where a man in a light-colored suit was sitting alone reading a newspaper. He put the newspaper down when they approached, stood up, and put out a hand.

"Mr. Wilson?"

Wilson nodded. It was a big hand, with spiky black hairs on the back and a couple of rings.

"Zapatero," the man said as they shook hands. He sat down again and waved at the other side of the table. Wilson sat down.

"Anything else, Chief?" the blond cop said.

"Yeah," Zapatero said, "go away."

The blond cop grinned and the two of them went away. Zapatero folded his newspaper carefully, put it to one side, and put his hand on his glass.

"You want a whiskey?"

"Thanks."

Zapatero snapped his fingers resoundingly and said, "Another J & B," to the barman Wilson supposed to be hovering somewhere behind him in the dark. His eyes were beginning to get used to the dimness. Zapatero had the kind of monumental Latin head the Romans used to put on their coins, prominent nose and forehead, thick lips set in a vaguely ironic, melancholy pout.

"Hot, isn't it?"

Wilson nodded agreement.

"This isn't official," Zapatero said with a twist of the lips that he might have thought served as a smile. "That's why I asked you here. And because it's the only place I know to get out of the heat."

The barman put a tall glass full of ice cubes on the table in front of him and poured it half full of whiskey. Wilson took a sip and winced.

"Tell me about this business," Zapatero said. "Nobody tells me anything."

As far as Wilson could see he was serious, so he told Zapatero everything he should have known anyway. When he was finished he spread his hands apologetically and said, "That's about it."

Zapatero scratched his nose with a little finger. "What kind of money has this Mr. Dantry got?"

"A lot."

"How much is that?"

"I don't know really," Wilson said uneasily.

"But he isn't famous for it, is he?"

"No," Wilson said. He wondered what Zapatero was getting at, and then he realized what it was. He wondered why he hadn't thought of it himself.

"What I mean is," Zapatero said in a tired voice, "there are quite a lot of American girls around. Apparently she didn't act like she was rich. So why her?"

"Yeah," Wilson said curtly. Zapatero irritated him, and it was irritating that he was already ahead of him.

84

Zapatero looked at him thoughtfully, then took a long drink. "Has anyone been in touch with you?"

"No."

"It's early yet," Zapatero said dully. "Anyone official?"

Wilson looked at him, thought about asking him what he meant and decided not to. Zapatero seemed absorbed in examining what was left of the ice cubes in his glass.

"No," Wilson said.

"If these people were to get in touch with you," Zapatero said slowly, facing him, "you'd let us know, wouldn't you?"

"What people?" Wilson said, lighting his pipe.

"The terrorists," Zapatero said wearily. He pronounced the word with a vague distaste and something that sounded a bit like irony.

Wilson took his time, puffing out little clouds of smoke across the table. "Would you really want me to? Dantry's got money. I suppose he's willing to pay. It might make things easier that way, for everybody. Don't you think?"

He offered Zapatero a thin tentative grin through the smoke.

Zapatero didn't smile back. He drank off the rest of his drink and snapped his fingers in the air. "Do you think so?"

"I get paid for a live client," Wilson said. He could feel the sweat under his arms in spite of the air-conditioning. The barman put two more glasses with ice in them on the table and poured out the whiskey. Zapatero tapped a cigarette on the table and waited until he had finished.

"That's not quite the point," he said.

Wilson took a sip of the fresh whiskey, nodded.

"You're here as a tourist," Zapatero said. "You should do some sightseeing."

"I have," Wilson said. "I've seen the cathedral." You make a wrong move and you fall off the board, he was thinking, and he probably already had. You offend one of these bastards and it's your ass.

"You should see the Gaudi buildings," Zapatero went on, "the church of the Sagrada Familia, Guell Park. Very interesting."

Wilson shifted his rear on the padded bunch and took the pipe out of his mouth. "Who do you think these people are?"

"There are a number of hypotheses," Zapatero said with a pained expression. "Too many hypotheses. What's your hypothesis, Mr. Wilson?"

Wilson shook his head.

Zapatero blew out a cloud of bluish smoke and shook his head. "This isn't New York, eh?" he said with a sour half smile.

"Chicago," Wilson muttered, "I'm from Chicago."

"Don't play the tough guy with me, Wilson," Zapatero said. "I'm too old for that kind of thing."

He picked up the newspaper and spread it out in front of him.

"You can go," he said. "I've got work to do."

Wilson stared at him, took another drink of his whiskey, and got up. There wasn't really anything else to do.

"Keep in touch," Zapatero said without looking up. He licked his forefinger and turned a page.

Valcarca telephoned a little before midnight. Wilson was drinking scotch and watching a movie about a girl who lived in the Swiss Alps with her drunken father who loved her, a sort of *Heidi* with a touch of sex and violence.

"The word is they think it's an anarchist group," Valcarca said. "That's unofficial, of course. But I've been checking into this and I think there are other possibilities."

Wilson found the right button on the remote control gadget and cut the sound on the TV. What looked like a toy train chugged past a string of mountains that would have looked nice on a chocolate bar wrapper.

"Like what?" he said.

"The Arabs, the French."

"The French?" Wilson said, reaching for his pipe.

"Listen," Valcarca said. "You remember the name Apocalypse? It's generally Islamic organizations that use names with religious connotation. A few months ago a group called the 'Call of Jesus Christ' was pulled in in Madrid. Supposedly Libyan-backed, but it turned out that the two top men—there were only seven— were working for the French Secret Service. The number-three man was working for our secret service. And the Islamic groups have never kidnapped women, even in Beirut. You follow me?"

86

"No," Wilson said. The commercials came on; a girl dived into an indoor swimming pool and came up smiling with a bottle of mouthwash. "What the hell have the French got to do with anything?"

"Disneyland," Valcarca said.

"Disneyland," Wilson repeated. With the whiskey he had drunk things seemed to lapse into a hazy harmless distance.

"They're going to build a Disneyland in Europe," Valcarca said, talking fast. "The project's been in the works for awhile. The choice of the site was between France and Spain, and France won. But in the last few months France has been having serious problems with Arab- and Iranian-backed terrorism, and the rumor is they're reconsidering. The Disney Corporation doesn't want that kind of trouble. You see?"

"I don't quite see the point," Wilson said, and heard a long, exaggerated sigh at the other end of the line.

"You Americans really are naive," Valcarca said patiently. "There are billions of dollars involved in the Disneyland deal, enough to make it what they call a *raison d'état*. The French Secret Service didn't hesitate to bump off those Greenpeace people in Australia. They're exporting the problem."

Valcarca stopped for breath, and Wilson watched the Swiss father sprawled in an armchair guzzling red wine from the bottle.

"You people have got technology," Valcarca said. "We've got sunshine and *paellas*. Our biggest single source of income is tourism. You understand now?"

The old man on the television screen dropped the bottle on the floor and looked as if he were about to have a heart attack.

"Who'd you get this from?" Wilson said.

"It's only a hypothesis," Valcarca said. "They don't talk about this kind of thing."

The telephone woke him out of a ragged dream. He fumbled for the water glass on the nightstand and took a long drink to rinse the raw whiskey taste out of his mouth while he put the phone to his ear. Haeflinger's voice said something he couldn't understand and probably didn't want to anyway.

"You know what time it is, Haeflinger?"

"It was ninety degrees at nine o'clock this morning," Haeflinger growled back. "There was a pile-up on the expressway and the elevator doesn't work. So don't give me any belly-aching. You probably just got out of the swimming pool."

"There isn't any swimming pool in this hotel. Besides it's three o'clock in the morning."

"Your wife wants to talk to you."

"Ex-wife," Wilson said, rubbing his eyes. The dark looked murky and speckled through the open window, and he could hear the whisper of car tires on the street below. "I don't wanta talk to her."

"I don't like her calling here."

"Why don't you tell her that? What do you want?"

"What do I want?" Haeflinger yelled. "I want results. Dantry's getting antsy. This thing's all over the papers. Dantry's people are talking about how we got the possibility of a Patty Hearst syndrome here."

"What the hell's that mean?" Wilson said, feeling like he really didn't want to know.

"That's when a rich cunt gets together with a terrorist with a big dick," Haeflinger said, and cackled for a while. Wilson rubbed the beard growing out on his chin, scratched the top of his head, and sighed. "Dantry's not very impressed with your work."

"The cops think it's anarchists," Wilson said, cutting him off.

"Anarchists? They still got anarchists over there?"

"Yeah. They got anarchists."

"What do they want?"

"I don't know. I got some contacts," Wilson lied. "I'm seeing a guy tomorrow."

"All right," Haeflinger said, "get your ass in gear. I got the feeling Dantry's been talking to the spooks. And if . . . if he cancels out on us it's going to be your ass. Understand?"

15

"So you moved in with him?" Wilson said.

"We couldn't stay at Marjorie's," Elizabeth said, shaking her head. "She used to go around after him emptying the ashtrays and wiping them out with a Kleenex. Juanjo couldn't stand her. She was jealous, I guess.

"We stayed a couple nights at his *pension*. The guy in the next room had his radio on all night, and you could hear it through the walls—they were like made of paper—and I met the landlord or the manager in the hall, and he acted like he was going to call the cops or something. It was really ridiculous. And Juanjo said what he wanted was for us to pay for another room, for me, and then he wouldn't have cared where we slept."

She glanced around the inside of the car for another beer, but didn't find one. There were empties on the floor in the back with a dribble of beer on the tops of the cans. The inside of the car was beginning to stink in the heat, of beer and tobacco and the smell of their own bodies, the smell of the road.

"We just walked around and talked a lot and looked at the buildings. There are a lot of beautiful buildings in Barcelona, you know. It wasn't really a sex thing. I just liked him, that's all."

She fixed her gaze on a bit of distant, hazy horizon and watched it for a while through the moving car window. Wilson shifted his grip on the steering wheel, licked his lips, and listened to the motor humming. After that long you kept listening to it and thinking it was going to stop any time.

"He told me how the fascists put his father in a work camp after the Civil War, and they used to make them carry sacks of quick lime on their bare backs in the sun. It'd burn their skin through the sacks."

"Juanjo's father was a Guardia Civil," Wilson said.

"How do you know?"

"I checked him out."

"Yeah, I suppose you did," she said coldly. She took out a cigarette and looked out the side window.

"He made me go see this movie called *Missing*," she said without looking at him. "I didn't want to see it. I knew Chile was a dictatorship and all that. I didn't want to see all that stuff about torture and all."

She lit the cigarette, and Wilson, keeping his eyes on the black highway with the dry, hot plain on both sides, thought: Maybe she's gonna explain it now, maybe she thinks she is explaining it. The only thing is it doesn't make any sense. Maybe she knows that too.

"There was one part, it wasn't very important, the two girls were in this place, it was some hotel or something, it was real nice, with this major or something like that from the American army, and the coup had already happened. The army guy knew that the boyfriend of one of the girls—that they already had him or that he was already dead. He knew that, and he was trying to put the make on the girls. He wasn't trying very hard, but he was nasty about it. The way they are, those kind of guys. He was sitting around getting drunk in this armchair, drinking whiskey, and the way he looked at the girl, it reminded me, sometimes there would be friends of my dad's drinking in the study with him, and they'd get drunk, and sometimes one of them would look at me just like that. Like they wouldn't do anything, but they were thinking about it. They wanted to fuck you, but they couldn't, and they kind of hated you for it, because they wanted to."

She looked at Wilson and said, "You probably wouldn't understand that."

"Why not?" Wilson said, and she shrugged, with a little slightly condescending smile. Wilson looked back at the road. There were road signs, clumps of sagebrush, pale-yellow dust. They passed a gang of Mexicans in a broken-down car, heading out to pick fruit someplace, Wilson thought. Brown faces packed together, slipping past like a dream. He had done that for a while, picked fruit here and there. Maybe you were better off like that, just drifting. But there was always a time when you got scared, when you had two dollars in your pocket and no job and no place to sleep. So you got a job and you got respectable. They gave you a license to carry a gun and you did respectable stuff like he did.

"The thing was," Elizabeth said, "he cared about things. Nobody else I ever knew ever cared about anything but themselves."

16

There was a hot dry wind blowing up through the city, off the Sahara the newspapers said, shaking the dusty leaves on the trees along the avenues. It blew the smog out of the air and left the sky a clear, piercing brilliant blue. Wilson had a dull hangover headache, and even with his sunglasses on the glare hurt his eyes.

He was sitting at a little round table on the street, surrounded by pink-skinned people from various countries sitting at similar little tables, with a newspaper in front of him and a small winged insect drowning slowly in the pool of sweat around the bottom of his beer glass. People kept walking by, endless waves of bodies simmering in the sunlight, and the treetops made moving shadows on the pavement. A gypsy kid about two feet tall was holding a dirty hand in front of Wilson's face and was not going to take it away until he put some money in it. Wilson looked into the small face that was frowning with the sullen patience of the undernourished, and they shared a moment of mutual incomprehension and mild hatred. Giving the gypsy kid money would not, Wilson realized, make himself a human being in his eyes. It would not make him feel good, it would even leave him with a vaguely rankling sense of shame. Not giving him anything would just leave him feeling like a shit. It was a loser's game either way. He put some coins in the kid's hand and looked in the other direction.

A tall transvestite in a short skirt sat down at another table and crossed his legs, showing a long slice of smooth thigh. He caught Wilson's eye and gave him a mocking smile. Wilson drank some beer and the sweat from the glass left a spot on his trousers. Wilson wondered what he was doing there and waited for the beer to do something for his hangover. He remembered how Haeflinger had told him once when he was angry with him about something that he couldn't find a fart with a bloodhound. Haeflinger was from Indiana, and Wilson had the idea that people from Indiana talked like that, but it didn't help much.

He had gone through all the motions, and Haeflinger had telexes out to morgues and police departments in all the likely European cities, so if the body turned up they would be first in with the news. There wasn't really anything to do but sit back and wait. But a good investigator, Wilson knew, kept on working, even when there was nothing to work on. A good investigator could always find another angle. A good investigator accumulated mountains of useless information on the idiotic supposition that eventually something would click. Because a good investigator believed, deep down, that things made sense. Wilson, deep down, was not that sure.

He paid for the beer and started walking. Eventually he would think of something; in the meantime he might just as well take a nap. He seemed to remember having read somewhere that many of the world's greatest thinkers had done some of their best thinking while they were asleep. A little way up the boulevard between the trees there were all kinds of animals and birds for sale, in cages stacked one on top of the other. He stopped and found himself staring at a prehistoric-looking lizard in a glass case. The lizard stood very still, on short splayed legs with skinny fingers, watching him with one brown eye. It looked as if it were waiting, waiting for something that it had been waiting for for a long time.

When he got back to the hotel the room was hot, even with the curtains drawn. They billowed with a gentle, swishing sound in the grayish dimness, and the roar of the traffic came up muffled from the street below. Wilson put a Thelonius Monk tape on the portable tape deck he had brought with him, took off his shoes, and lay down on top of the covers. He was almost asleep when the telephone rang.

"Wilson," the voice at the other end said. He knew it was a Spanish voice because it made his name sound like "Geelson."

He said, "Yes."

"This is Juan," the voice said, and for a moment Wilson thought it was Elizabeth's boyfriend calling up to solve his case for him. "I'm just calling to say fuck you. Thanks to you my stomach's one big bruise and it hurts when I piss and . . . So thanks a lot, okay?"

It was Jilguero. He was talking too fast for Wilson to make out all the words, but he got the general idea.

"What are you talking about?" he said mildly.

"I mean, asshole, that they took me down to the station, and we had a little conversation, and I lost. So how'd they get on to me if it wasn't through you, huh, private detective? You get the picture? That's all I wanted to say, just fuck you."

Wilson heard the phone slam down at the other end and hung up his own. He sat up on the edge of the bed with his chin in his hand and looked at the floor for a while. Then he took a quick shower and changed his clothes. He took a wad of bills out of the dresser drawer and put it in the front pocket of his trousers and went out.

When he came out of the hotel the tops of the palm trees were shaking clumsily over endless streams of cars. He walked the couple of blocks to the nearest *Metro* station and down the yellow steps past a poster for a new American horror movie. It was late afternoon and the station was crowded with people walking fast and looking hot and irritable. He put some money into a slot and went through a turnstile. There was a tiny glassed-in bar on the other side, opposite a newsstand. He took the only unoccupied stool and ordered a coffee and sat listening to a radio station with a hysterical disc jockey, turned up loud. A skinny African with a long sad face came through the open doorway and showed him some wooden elephants.

Wilson paid for the coffee and went down the stairs to the platform. He took the train to the first stop that had a connection to another line and walked down the tunnel between the two lines. When he got to the end of the tunnel he turned around and walked back, checking the faces. When he was about halfway down he stopped and walked back again, taking his time.

The guy who was following him was short, with dark hair and a close-cropped beard. He was going to keep on walking. Wilson stepped in front of him and said, "You new on the job?"

The guy looked up at him with a nervous twist of a smirk to his mouth, shrugged, and tried to go around him. Wilson edged him against the wall, blocking him with his bulk, not so as any of the people hurrying past would have noticed.

"You wanna show me some identification?" Wilson said. He could feel his face getting red, and it occurred to him that he was probably making a mistake and he didn't need any more mistakes.

"I don't know what you're talking about," the guy said. His smirk got a little more obnoxious, so he was a cop for sure, probably thinking about how much fun it would be taking Wilson in, maybe going over him with a rubber billy club or whatever they used.

"Tell your asshole of a boss not to lean on people I talk to," Wilson said, and started walking. All the way down the tunnel he had the feeling somebody was going to come up behind him and put a hand on his shoulder. Nobody did.

Wilson went up to street level. It was a relief to come up from underground, and the hot wind felt kind of good on his face. He hailed a cab, gave the driver Jilguero's address, and watched the cars behind them until he got tired of it. Fucking stupid, he thought. It would have been easy enough to shake the twerp, there wasn't any point in talking to him, no point at all, and probably a few good reasons not to.

The traffic was heavy and snarled. After twenty minutes Wilson told the driver to drop him at a *Metro* station on the line that went out to Jilguero's neighborhood. When he came out of the *Metro* he went into a small bar that smelled of cooking grease and drank a beer, looking out at the street, six lanes wide and clogged with traffic, between immense, grim apartment buildings.

Jilguero's girlfriend kept the chain on the door when she opened it, and when she recognized Wilson she tried to close it again, but he already had his foot in the crack. He hit the door with his shoulder, putting his weight behind it. The door screeched and fell open, tearing the end of the chain out of the wall, knocking the girlfriend back across the room.

"Excuse me," Wilson said.

"Get outa here!" she yelled, and seemed to be looking around for something to throw at him. The walls were a sickly pale green, covered with unframed prints of strange-looking paintings and posters of Marilyn Monroe and James Dean. The furniture was made of plastic, with skinny metal legs.

"Take it easy," Wilson said. "I'm not here to hurt anybody." He crossed the room to the bedroom, hoping she wouldn't hit from behind. Jilguero was sitting up in bed in a Wittgenstein T-shirt, with a pile of comic books and a case of beer on the floor beside him. He sat up a little straighter when he saw Wilson, and made a face.

"What the fuck do you want? You wanna beat me up too?"

Wilson put out both hands, palms forward, in a conciliatory gesture. "Listen. I'm sorry about this, believe me."

The girlfriend leaned against the door jamb, arms folded over her thin chest, and looked at him with evident hatred.

"What happened?" Wilson said.

"I told you what happened," Jilguero said. "What the hell do you want to know for anyway?"

"Look, I know this was my fault. I'm sorry. I'm a fuckup, okay? But I don't get it."

"No?" Jilguero drank the rest of his beer and put the empty in the case. "Bring me a cold one, would you, baby?" he said to the girlfriend. "And don't give him one."

"So you don't get it," he said to Wilson. "Well, I'll explain it to you. I got a record. In this country most everybody with any balls has got a record, had a record. Because it was supposed to be wiped off the books with the amnesty of 1977. I told 'em that, and the cop said, 'We gonna take your amnesty and shove it up your ass till it comes out of your nose.' You get it now? Like somebody forgot to take my name off the computer."

The girlfriend gave him a beer and he drank some. "You get it?"

"What'd they ask you?"

"About Elizabeth Dantry. Same as you. So why don't you get outa here now?"

Wilson shrugged. "What else did they ask you?"

"If I belonged to any organization. I told 'em the Barcelona Football Club. They didn't think that was funny. I was lucky though. They could've given me the antiterrorist law, taken me off to Madrid and worked me over for a week. I don't know why they didn't. When they let me out this cop asked me if I wanted to work for them. Pass them a little information." Jilguero shook his head disgustedly.

"What'd you say?"

Jilguero glanced at him sharply, tightening his lips. "What the fuck am I going to say? Look, I haven't got any reason to like you and I got a couple of good reasons not to, so why don't you just fuck off, huh?"

"Look," Wilson said quietly, "you know Elizabeth. I'm just doing a job, I'm just trying to find her, that's all."

"This guy's an asshole, Juan," the girlfriend said from the doorway.

"You know Elizabeth," Wilson said gently, "you been to bed with her . . ."

"What?" the girlfriend said disgustedly.

Jilguero waved his arms unconvincingly, like some guy in an Italian movie, and said, "I don't know what you're talking about."

"I'd like your help," Wilson said.

Jilguero shook his head. "Go on, get outa here."

Wilson took the wad of bills out of his pocket and tossed it onto the foot of the bed. Jilguero stared at it and said, "What's that?"

"Money," Wilson said.

"Yeah, that I can see."

"Pick it up," Wilson said. "Count it."

"Don't," the girlfriend said. She was looking at it the way people look at the exhibits in the reptile house at the zoo. Jilguero didn't move.

"There's a lot of things you can do with money," Wilson said philosophically.

"What's your game?" Jilguero said.

"Leave it, Juan," the girlfriend said.

"There's a guy named Juanjo that was mixed up with Elizabeth

97

before she disappeared. That's why they picked you up. They thought you were him.

"I don't know anybody named Juanjo."

"Everybody knows somebody named Juanjo," Wilson said. "The other part is to let me know they should talk to me. Dantry'll pay. No problems, no fuckups."

"I don't know anything about this," Jilguero said.

"I suppose they pulled you in for a reason, didn't they? Talk to your old friends. Get the word out."

He took the money off the bed and held it up in one hand, as if he were feeling its weight.

"There's a hundred and twenty-five thousand pesetas here. If somebody else wants a piece of it, you work that out between yourselves. If you get me what I want."

Jilguero just stared at him sullenly, thinking about it, and not wanting to admit it.

"We're not talking about fingering anybody. You just do everybody involved a favor. What do you think happens if the cops find her first?"

He put the money in his pocket. "Think it over. Oh, and don't call me at the hotel. I'll call you tomorrow and give you another number."

Jilguero just sat there. Wilson nodded to him, and the girlfriend followed him to the door.

"You're a son of a bitch," she said.

"Yeah," Wilson said. "I know." You could take it as a compliment in a way.

17

Wilson gave the George V Hotel in Paris as a forwarding address when he checked out of the hotel. He didn't really think anybody would believe it, but he didn't want to pass up the chance to cause them a little extra trouble, and the girl at the information desk had told him it was the best hotel in Paris. If they had taken the trouble to have him followed they might very likely have put a tap on his phone as well, and that meant that he had to move. They would find him again, of course, but it would take them another day or two, between finding where he was and putting a new tap on. There wasn't really any other way to play it.

He took a taxi to the central train terminal in Sants, where there was a direct train to the airport. It was one of those horrifyingly modern, sprawling train stations with escalators and lots of indecipherable signs and scruffy-looking kids with deep suntans sitting around on the floor leaning on their backpacks. He went down to a platform and got on a train loading for Seville, walked through the train past people struggling with luggage and small children, got off and took the escalator back up to the station. A public address system announced something in several different languages, all of them incomprehensible. It was impossible to pick out anybody following him in that milling mass of people, and the shoulder strap of his bag was beginning to dig painfully into his shoulder. He took an escalator down to the *Metro* station, paid and walked down the platform and took the escalator going up at a run, then crossed the station and took another cab.

The hotel he had picked out of a guidebook was not much different from the one he had left, carpets and aerosol smell, a whisper of canned music in the elevators and people that looked with distaste at the sweat stains under his arms. The room was on the eighth floor, with a view of Tibidabo Mountain at the top of the city. When the sun started going down they lit up the church and the amusement park next to it. You could hardly tell them apart.

He called Haeflinger's office and told the answering machine the hotel telephone number. Then he called Valcarca's newspaper and was told Valcarca wasn't there. He didn't really want to talk to him anyway. Jilguero he could leave until the next day. He wouldn't have anything to tell him yet anyway, if he ever did.

He took a long shower and then sat on the bed in his undershorts smoking a joint and watching the sky get dark and the lights come on. The lights thinned out toward Tibidabo, there were patches on the hills where nobody had got around to building anything yet, and Wilson found that oddly comforting, even kind of pretty. He took the little notebook out of his suitcase and wrote in a rough estimate of the day's expenses. Then he drew three columns and wrote in, "Anarchists 1, Arabs 1, French 0," looked at it, and giggled for a while.

The hotel bar was like some cocktail lounge in Cleveland or Milwaukee, dark with plush booths and dim-lit tables, men in business suits talking too loud and elegant-looking women whispering. All of them looked better dressed and better looking and wealthier than Wilson did. He sat at the bar drinking beer and sneaking glances at women's legs, listening to the syrupy piped-in music and getting gloomily high. When he served his third beer the barman asked nonchalantly if he might be interested in a woman. Hotel employees frequently asked him that kind of question. Almost the only place they didn't was in Ramada Inns, which are owned by the Mormons.

"No," Wilson said. "Sheep. I like sheep."

The barman smiled unpleasantly and went away. Wilson knew he had to finish his beer and get out of there before he started thinking about it and ended up with some beautiful whore in expensive lingerie running down the list of the routines she could do.

Wilson rolled another joint in the room, put on an Ornette Coleman tape, and stretched out on the bed, opening up the first volume of *The Decline and Fall of the Roman Empire*. He had bought the twelve volumes of the paperback edition at a used book store in Chicago a few months before, and brought the first two volumes with him with the idea that he might have plenty of time to kill. The footnotes distracted him, they were long and often more interesting than the text itself, so that you lost your place and had to keep turning back pages and starting over again, but he found that he liked dipping into it. There was something disturbing about it, the suspicion that it might have been one tremendous practical joke, that it was impossible for one person to have written all that stuff, let alone researched it, but he liked the way it went on and on, all those emperors and generals whose names everybody had forgotten murdering each other one after the other, the tremendous futility of it. It reminded him of what the Hindus, or maybe it was the Buddhists, said about the pointless repetition of history, especially when he was stoned.

He was in a deep sleep when the phone rang, making horrible noises until his hand found it and Haeflinger growled, "The spooks got the jump on you, Wilson."

"Huh?" Wilson said. He recognized Haeflinger's voice, but in the dark, the strange shapes in the unfamiliar room, he had no idea where he was or why.

"What have you been doing over there, sunbathing?"

Wilson found the water glass with his free hand and poured it over his head.

"Huh?" Haeflinger demanded.

"They got more manpower than I have," Wilson said, gasping.

"That's for goddam sure," Haeflinger said unpleasantly. "Okay, listen, I got it set up for you. You're gonna make the change, you carry the money."

"Thanks," Wilson said, "I appreciate that."

101

"Right. Talk to that asshole Schumacher. He's got the dope."

"What's the story?"

"Talk to Schumacher. What'd you change hotels for? Didn't like the toilet paper?"

"I figured they might have a tap on my phone."

"Who? The cops?"

"Yeah."

"They talk to you?"

"Yeah."

"What'd they say?"

Wilson tried to think of something Zapatero had said that he could afford to tell Haeflinger.

"Not much," he said.

"Got their thumbs up their asses, right?" Haeflinger said cheerfully. "Okay, you'll have to get the money from the bank, the *Banco Central*, got it? In the morning. Talk to Schumacher. Is it morning there yet?"

"Yeah," Wilson said looking at his travel clock, "four o'clock in the morning."

"Right. Call me as soon as you get her. Doesn't matter what time. You can call me at home. As soon as you get that little cunt you get her on the first plane out and you get her ass home to daddy. All right?"

"Right," Wilson said, and hung up. He set the alarm on his travel clock for eight o'clock. His eyes had got used to the darkness, but the room still gave him the creeps.

Schumacher was sitting outside, in a little plaza down the street from the consulate. He had a glass of hot water in front of him with a teabag and a lemon in it and a saucer on top. He was wearing a seersucker jacket with wide blue stripes and beige trousers, which managed to make him look even more forlorn than before. He stood up when Wilson got there, and they shook hands.

"I don't think we should talk here," Schumacher said into Wilson's ear.

"Aren't you going to drink your tea?"

Schumacher looked at the glass and said, "I already paid for it."

102

They walked down the street toward the port. It was a little after nine and the sidewalk was crowded with sullen-looking civil servants heading for the Ministry of Labor building on the other side of the street. Schumacher kept close to Wilson's shoulder, rubbing his hands together nervously.

"You'll need a briefcase," he said.

"A briefcase?"

"To put the money in."

"Right," Wilson said. To put the money in. They crossed the wide avenue in front of the main post office. On the other side there were palm trees lining the wide promenade that ran along the shore. A jogger came pounding by with calf muscles like paperweights.

"There's a little problem come up," Schumacher said hesitantly, glancing out to sea past the clutter of boats, masts and cranes. The water sloshed dark and oily against the metal sides of big gray ships.

"We've been doing a little checking, and it looks from our information like you were in some demonstrations with a group called Vietnam Veterans Against the War. Now I know that was a long time ago, and you fellows had kind of a rough time over there, but I suppose you know that was a Commie front group?"

"No, they didn't tell me," Wilson said. "You guys have got a lot of information, haven't you?"

"It just came in at the last minute," Schumacher said apologetically.

"I thought you were against making deals with terrorists?"

Schumacher winced and then grinned feebly. He looked as if he had been out in the sun that weekend. His face was an unnatural, phosphorescent pink.

"We're not involved in this officially," he said. "It's your show."

"Who are these guys?"

"We don't know. But we've got a pretty good idea who they might be."

"I bet you do," Wilson said, kicking a stone out of his path. There were a couple of plastic cups bouncing on the water close in to shore and a faint dirty film on the blue sky. It was going to be hot again.

103

"Ask for Mr. Verduro at the *Banco Central*," Schumacher said. "He'll have the money for you. You'll have to take along the briefcase. The bank closes at two."

"And then?"

There were yachts anchored to that part of the pier. They came up beside one that was about sixty feet long, all varnished wood and brass fittings, everything polished and in its place. There didn't seem to be anybody on board.

"Get a black plastic briefcase," Schumacher said, staring dreamily at the yacht. "Beautiful boat, isn't it? Be at the Ritz Hotel, in the lobby, at nine o'clock. With the briefcase, of course. Someone will tell you where to go. It'll be a bar somewhere. Take a cab, don't stop to phone or go to the toilet or anything. When they deliver the girl our man will call you where you are and you hand over the briefcase."

"How do they know I haven't just got a sandwich in it?"

"You show him the money," Schumacher said, "in the men's room. Then he'll phone his people and give the go ahead."

"Where are they delivering the girl?"

A group of Japanese tourists lined up to take snapshots of the boat. Schumacher raised his eyebrows significantly and they began walking again.

"Another bar, I suppose," Schumacher said. "That's our end. Our man will say, 'This is Archie' when he calls. That's how you'll know he's on the up and up."

"I'll need a gun," Wilson said. "The other guy'll have a gun."

"A gun?" Schumacher said, frowning at his shoes. "Yes, I suppose you will."

"A revolver preferably, thirty-eight, short barrel."

"I'll see about it," Schumacher said, squinting at the water, hesitating. "I suppose you've done this sort of thing before?"

"Sure," Wilson said, rubbing the sweat on the back of his neck. "Lots of times."

18

Wilson bought a black, hard plastic briefcase in a big department store called the *Corte Ingles*, and then walked around the Plaza Catalunya to the bank. A kid with long hair was doing a plausible version of the Assumption of the Virgin in colored chalks on the pavement. People stood around watching and a few dropped coins into an old cookie tin. A little farther on a small group of men were gathered around an up-ended crate playing something with three cards that looked like a variation on the shell game, with shabby lookouts posted in both directions to watch out for the cops.

Mr. Verduro was an unfriendly-looking man with a small mustache and an executive paunch. He took Wilson into his private office and put the money into the briefcase in neat stacks while Wilson sat in an imitation leather chair and tried not to look. When he had finished putting the money in the briefcase he gave Wilson a receipt to sign: $200,000 at 126.5 pesetas to the dollar, minus costs and commission. They took a good commission.

Wilson took a taxi back to the hotel and had the briefcase put in the hotel safe. He had to fill out a slip at the desk, and he hesitated for a moment over the line marked contents, then wrote in "Cash."

The desk clerk on duty was young, he wore a blue blazer with the hotel's name on the pocket and looked as if he had been cleaned and pressed along with his clothes. He said he would have to take a look, lifted the lid a couple inches, and then closed it hastily.

"It's strictly confidential," he said, blushing.

"I hope so," Wilson said.

He took a shower and had lunch in the hotel dining room. It was modern and elegant, with thick white tablecloths and flowers in glass vases on the tables, and almost empty. He had a plate of grilled shrimp, followed by a thick steak with mushroom sauce, and drank a bottle of chilled white wine. For dessert he ate a big dish of nutty-flavored ice cream with walnuts and whipped cream on it. Then he sat there for a while, smoking and spilling ash on the tablecloth.

He went back to the room and sat in front of the television for awhile after lunch, alternating between two cop shows that were more or less interchangeable. Then he lay down on the bed and looked at the gold leaf thing around the light in the ceiling.

He was sweating when he woke up, with the image still fresh in his mind of a hunchbacked cockroach lurching after him through the Paris *Metro* and the fuzzy memory of a number of other things that had happened to him in his dreams, all bad. He threw some water on his face and neck and then sat on the bed for a moment looking at the view. Then he picked up the phone and called Chicago.

"Listen," he said when Haeflinger came on the line, "this thing stinks."

"What's the problem, Wilson?" Haeflinger said. It was morning there, and Haeflinger sounded a little less nasty than usual. "You got cold feet?"

"It doesn't make any sense. I mean, what did these guys want to risk going through the consulate for?"

"I thought you said your phone was tapped?"

"That was the other one," Wilson said, wondering for a second if they hadn't had time to put another one, and deciding it was just too late to worry about. "I moved. How do I know they're not going to put a tail on me—or one of those electronic gadgets they've got?"

"They're not gonna do anything like that," Haeflinger said.

106

"They don't want any dead bodies. They've had enough trouble with hostages, right?" He chuckled unpleasantly.

"I just don't wanta get set up," Wilson muttered.

"You want me to come over and hold your hand, Wilson?" Haeflinger sneered. "You're a tough guy, right? You're a veteran. This is what you get paid for, you know?"

"Forget it," Wilson said. He put the phone down and went into the bathroom to take another shower.

When he came out of the shower he called room service and ordered a beer. He thought he would have to take it easy on the drinks from then on, one beer, two at the most.

A waiter brought him up his beer, and a few minutes later a bellhop knocked on the door and gave him a package. Wilson tipped him too much, opened the package, and took out the pistol. He put on the Ornette Coleman tape and turned the sound on the television off and held the pistol in his hand getting the feel of it. It was gunmetal blue with a wood handle and a two-inch barrel. He knocked out the chamber, looked down the barrel, and checked the action. He got some toilet paper from the bathroom and pushed it down the barrel with a pencil. Then he sat down and loaded it. He sat for a while watching the soundless images on the television screen and holding the gun in his lap, thought about smoking a joint and decided against it. It got dark late at that time of the year. The buildings outside the window looked hard and ugly in the smudgy sunshine.

Wilson dialed Jilguero's number and a woman's voice answered. She said, "Fuck off" when he told her who he was, but she didn't hang up.

"Is Juan there?"

"No," she said. "Why don't you go back to your own country?"

"I'd like to," Wilson said. He could feel a tickly sensation creeping up between his legs. The travel clock by the bed read seven twenty-five. "Let me give you my number, in case he wants to call."

"What's he going to want to call you for?"

"Just in case," Wilson said. He gave her the number and he guessed she wrote it down. It wouldn't make any difference. Jilguero would never call him. But if you're a professional, Wilson thought, you cover all the angles. Besides, it was something to do.

107

At eight o'clock Wilson put on his blue suit, sat around a little longer, and then went down, got the briefcase out of the safe, and caught a taxi. The twilight was just coming on when he got out of the cab in front of the Ritz, and he caught a glimpse of blurry pink sky down at the end of the long wide avenue. A doorman in a gold braided tunic held the door for him, and he thought for a second of statesmen you see on the TV news getting out of limousines with their briefcases. The difference was that there was no one at the top of the steps waiting to shake hands with him.

The Ritz was not really the place to go any more, and probably hadn't been for the last thirty years or so. The best hotels were in the upper, northwest corner of the city now, tall sleek structures with smoked-glass windows. The Ritz was for rich people who didn't know what was going on. Wilson had heard somebody explaining this in the bar in his hotel and supposed it was probably true. There were two adjoining lobbies, big vases full of flowers, people walking through looking fastidious, women in hats. The walls were creamy white with fluted half columns, niches and woodwork like the icing on a wedding cake. Wilson stood for a while shifting the briefcase from hand to hand and then sat down on a straight embroidered chair, sitting a little forward so as not to jam the gun into his back.

He sat there for what seemed quite a while, until a waiter asked him if he were Mr. Wilson and gave him a note when he said that he was. It was on hotel notepaper, the name of a bar and the address, printed in big letters. The waiter was still standing there so Wilson gave him a tip.

It was dark when he went outside. He got into another taxi, told the driver the address, and leaned back and watched the lights go by. They were going up toward the hills, more or less back the same way he had come. There was traffic, but it was moving fast. It would be easy enough to follow him, he guessed. He wasn't sure that was bad.

The driver took a sharp turn into a side street, braked and edged along while two kids in sleeveless leather jackets with writing on the backs took their time getting out of the way and then made farting noises as they went by. Wilson had a rough idea where they were, but didn't know that part of the city. The streets were cobbled, with cars parked on both sides up on the narrow pavement, and the

108

buildings looked old and rundown, with small balconies with metal railings, windows open and the racket of television sets coming out of them. The driver took a couple more turns and double parked.

"It's down there," he said while Wilson got his money out, pointing at an alleyway. It was about two meters wide, with lights spilling onto it out of the windows and a couple of black lampposts in the middle. About halfway down the alley there was what was supposed to look like an English pub sign, a picture of a pig with a ring in its nose. A nice quiet place, Wilson thought.

He paid the taxi driver and walked down the alley with briefcase in his left hand and his right hand free. There was no one around that he could see, and hardly any noise except the faint hum from the smoke extractor on the front of the bar. The far end of the alley opened onto what looked like another empty street or perhaps one end of a quiet plaza. Wilson supposed he made a pretty easy shot from the street behind him. He kept close to the wall and listened to his shoes clicking on the cement. The bar had a shiny wood door at street level and a little window too high up to see through. He walked in, and nobody shot him.

There were three or four steps up from the doorway to the level of the bar, a wooden banister, a short bar on his left, and a small room decorated according to somebody's idea of an English pub, with captain's chairs around low tables and fox hunting prints on the walls. Four men in suits were at the bar, eating popcorn and talking too loud, and two couples were sitting together in the far corner. Wilson sat down where he could watch the door and put the briefcase on the floor, between himself and the wall. He ordered a beer from a silver-haired barman in a black suit and started filling his pipe.

The guy was easy enough to recognize. He looked North African, or maybe from Syria, Lebanon, someplace like that. He was wearing a loose cotton jacket over a black polo shirt, and he walked straight to Wilson's table. He smiled once before he sat down. He had full lips, a deep chest and round muscular shoulders, a bulge under his left shoulder where he was probably keeping his gun. He looked like the sort of guy you would send out to pick up $200,000.

The waiter came over again, and the Arab ordered a whiskey. He folded his hands while he waited. When the waiter had poured out the whiskey he touched the glass with his fingertips, moving it a fraction of an inch to one side. His hands were broad and well kept, and he moved them with a sort of exaggerated care, as if he didn't like getting them dirty.

"I'll have to see the merchandise," he said, smiling again. He spoke good Spanish with hardly any accent, just a little too carefully. "I suppose they explained the arrangements?"

Wilson nodded. "I'll go first, if you don't mind."

The toilet was around the corner, behind a door at the end of the bar. It was small and clean and smelled of disinfectant. Wilson took the revolver out of the back of his trousers, put it in his jacket pocket, and kept his hand on it. He leaned against the white-tiled wall next to the urinal with the briefcase in his left hand and tried to look casual in case somebody else came in.

The Arab didn't look surprised to see the hand in Wilson's pocket. He shut the door behind him, and Wilson put the briefcase on the washbasin and clicked it open. Then he reached behind the Arab and locked the door, hoping nobody would get an urge to piss in the next couple of minutes. The Arab turned over the stacks of bills, picked up and flipped through a couple, bit his lip and smiled in spite of himself.

"That's all right," he said. Wilson nodded and the Arab unlocked the door and went out.

Wilson closed the briefcase, stuck the gun into the back of his trousers, and waited a minute. When he went back into the bar he tried keeping the briefcase between himself and the wall. Most people don't take their briefcases with them to the toilet. The Arab was just putting down the telephone at the bar. They sat down, and the Arab took a sip of his whiskey.

Nobody had said how long it was going to take. They would have to get her into a car, drive her to the place, maybe make some more phone calls. It would take longer if they had her someplace outside of town, or if the traffic was tied up.

The Arab sat with his eyes half closed, sipping the whiskey and smoking Benson & Hedges cigarettes. Wilson kept an eye on his hands. The two couples left and a few more people came in. It wasn't a very lively place. The waiter gave them a dish of popcorn.

After a while they both knew it was taking too long. The Arab's glass was empty. He signaled the waiter and pointed at Wilson's glass, questioning him with his eyes. We're in the same line of work, Wilson thought suddenly. It didn't mean anything, he just hadn't thought of it before.

He pointed to the Arab's glass, and asked for the same. One whiskey he could handle. The waiter brought fresh glasses and poured the whiskey over the ice.

The telephone made a discreet buzzing noise. The waiter was mixing up some kind of cocktail in an aluminum shaker and took his time getting to it. The Arab straightened up in his chair, their eyes met, and he gave Wilson a cool, seductive smile. Wilson kept on watching the Arab's hands, so he didn't see the waiter pick up the phone, just heard the buzzing stop and then a voice, raised but only a little, calling "Mr. Wilson."

He picked up the briefcase, feeling slightly silly about it, walked to the bar, leaned an elbow on it, and picked up the phone.

"Wilson? This is Archie. There's been no delivery. Repeat. There's been no delivery. Is your man there?"

"Yeah," Wilson said quietly. "How long have you been waiting?" He kept his voice down and his expression blank. So it was blown. The briefcase was leaning uncomfortably against his leg. The Arab was watching him, lighting a cigarette with a flashy lighter.

"A little over an hour. They told me twenty minutes."

"Maybe they had a flat tire," Wilson said. "Call me back in half an hour."

It was blown, he thought. You had to make sure, but he knew it was already blown.

He picked up the briefcase, walked back to the table, sat down, put the briefcase on the floor. The Arab's right hand wasn't on the table anymore. It had been, but it wasn't anymore. The Germans had a word like that for a second, *augenblick,* the blink of an eye. Everybody has to blink some time.

"She isn't there yet," Wilson said pointlessly.

"I'm sorry, Mr. Wilson," the Arab said softly.

Wilson had figured him for a shoulder holster. The bulge was still there under his armpit. His jacket had big floppy pockets, he could have had a small automatic there. You wouldn't have noticed it. It could have been a bluff, but he didn't think it was.

111

"Pass me the briefcase," the Arab said. His voice was steady, soothing, like somebody trying to coax a child into doing the reasonable thing.

Wilson passed him the briefcase. The Arab stood up carefully and sidestepped to the door with his hand in his jacket pocket. He didn't look very natural, but he didn't seem to care. When he reached the steps he started moving fast.

Wilson was already up, running for the door and pulling at the gun in the waistband of his trousers. He saw the barman raise his eyebrows, freeze with the cocktail shaker in his two hands, heard the banister creak in pain as he put his weight on it to jump the stairwell. The Arab might have been waiting for him to come out, but there wasn't really much he could do about it. He crouched as he went through the door, bracing himself to hit the wall on the other side of the alley. The muggy street air hit his face and for a second he expected the thud of a bullet into him. He hit the wall and bounced off still standing.

The Arab was running toward the far end of the alley, in rubber-soled shoes that made a flopping sound on the cement. Wilson came off the wall running too, swearing to himself. Run, you fat bastard, he was thinking, because if you don't get that money back Haeflinger's never gonna let you forget it.

The briefcase slowed the Arab down a little, but not enough, and he was going to reach the end of the alley in about two more steps. Shoot off his kneecap, Wilson thought, trying to work up a little hate, just enough to squeeze the trigger. He had shot people before—or thought he had—but in the war you never saw their faces. He took two fast shots at his legs. The Arab pulled the gun out of his pocket and Wilson flopped on the pavement and heard about half a clip chipping the concrete. Not as good as he looks, Wilson thought, and shot him in the leg, but he didn't go down. If he keeps on shooting you're going to have to kill him, Wilson thought. So go ahead, kill him. That's what they pay you for.

He heard a hollow crack on the pavement and saw the briefcase skidding toward him. The top sprang open and stacks of money began plopping out onto the cement. The shadow of the Arab limped around the corner.

Wilson stood up and realized there were people behind him,

yelling things he didn't bother to try to understand, but keeping their distance. His hands were shaking when he started jamming the money back into the briefcase. What wouldn't fit he stuffed into the side pockets of his jacket, then he got out of there. He didn't feel like talking to anybody.

19

There was a tour bus taking up about half of the parking lot in front of the café. Old people were still climbing out of it, squinting in the sun and taking pictures of one another. When Wilson cut the engine the sound of it kept on echoing in his head. You could see a river down below in the gorge, running clear and fast.

"All that water makes me want to piss," Wilson said, but Elizabeth didn't laugh. "We can get some coffee," he said.

The sun was too bright, Wilson thought as they walked across the parking lot, and the old people's voices were too loud and shrill. They wore pastel colors and sun visors with advertising on them, and a lot of them looked as if they might keel over at any moment.

The café had photos of Arizona's natural monuments hung on knotty pine walls, big windows so you could watch the cars going by on the highway, waitresses in starched aprons bustling around with glass coffeepots. When Wilson came back from the toilet there were two cups on the table, and Elizabeth was resting the side of her face on one hand, looking out the window. Wilson put some cream in his coffee and stirred it with a dented spoon.

"I suppose you just think I'm a nut, don't you?" she said.

"What difference does it make what I think?"

"None," she said, and looked out the window again.

For the last twenty miles or so there had been signs along the highway telling them they were almost to California and how wonderful it was going to be, and Wilson was still wondering what was going to happen at the border. Maybe it would be better, he thought, to just get it over with. He ought to call Haeflinger; there were probably a lot of things he ought to do.

"You were telling me how you moved in with Juanjo," he said, stirring his coffee some more.

"He said that the way things are now, they use the media to turn people into idiots. We used to watch the politicians and the newscasters on television with the sound off, just watch their faces move. He said they got so used to talking shit they didn't even realize they were doing it any more. Telling the same lies over and over again until nobody bothers to think about them. He said whatever you do they can turn it to their advantage, because they control information, so they control reality. Nothing's real if it doesn't get on television, you know? But nothing on television is quite real. He said what we had to do was use their own methods against them. Turn it around on them. You understand?"

"Not exactly," Wilson said. "What's the point?"

She drank some coffee and made a face. "Well, there wasn't any, was there? But I didn't know that then."

She opened up her bag, found a fresh pack of cigarettes, and put it on the table. "It seems like a long time ago now."

"Who else was there in this?" Wilson said quietly.

"Nobody. At least that's what I thought. Now I don't know. He talked a little bit about groups he'd been in, but not much, he said it had all fallen apart. I didn't ask him things like that. It was like too . . . intimate. I thought he'd tell me when he wanted to. Like I knew he'd been in jail, but he didn't talk about it."

"How'd you know?"

"Just things that he said. And he used to have bad dreams at night. He used to sleep curled up against me and sometimes he'd make kind of moaning noises and twist around like he was . . . I remember we had a dog when I was a kid, he was a big dog, a kind of setter, and he used to sleep stretched out in front of the fire,

115

sometimes he'd start whimpering in his sleep and move his legs like he was running. He wouldn't wake up, he'd just stop after a while and go on sleeping. Juanjo was like that."

The waitress came around and poured them some more coffee and went away, her apron crackling as she moved.

"He had this gun. I don't remember exactly when it was that he showed it to me. He wanted me to realize that it was important. To him having that gun was a big thing, and he wanted me to know that he wouldn't just show it to anybody. It seemed a little silly to me. I mean, if you grow up in the West you're around guns all the time. I used to go out with my brothers and shoot up beer cans and things, a gun was never any big deal to me. He said he'd show me how to use it, and he was surprised, kind of disappointed, I guess, when I told him I knew. We were talking about the thing then, just talking. At first it was like one of those fantasies that's fun to talk about but you know you're never going to do. But Juanjo was serious. That's what I liked about him, I guess, he was serious about things.

"We were staying with these friends of Juanjo's, and when we decided . . . to do it, well, we couldn't stay there, so I told him about the money in the bank. I didn't want to touch that money, but there wasn't any other way."

"Why didn't you want to touch the money?" Wilson said.

"Because it was my parents'. I wanted to leave them behind. Not just because of Juanjo. I've wanted to for a long time, I don't know how long. As long as I kept on living on their money they'd still have something on me. I didn't want to have any more to do with them."

Wilson raised his eyebrows.

"Because I don't like them," she said. Spots of color had come out on her cheeks and her eyes sparkled with vehemence. "They're selfish and stupid and pretentious, the only thing they ever think about is 'I want.' I know they're part of my past and I've got their blood and their genes, their DNA and all that, but I don't really like them, that's all."

She took a cigarette from the pack and tapped it on the table with a brisk movement, three times, and put it in her mouth.

116

"So anyway," she said in a dull voice, "I told Juanjo I had this money in the bank that we could use to get a place."

"He didn't know . . . that you had money? That your parents had money, I mean?"

"No."

"Until it came out in the papers?"

She looked at him sharply, shrugged, and glanced out the window, at a shiny pickup running fast down the highway.

"What was he doing for money?"

"He was on unemployment. It was gonna run out, I think."

The old people were lining up in the parking lot, climbing slowly onto the tour bus one by one. Wilson wondered if he would end up doing something like that. It was hard to imagine, but you ended up doing a lot of things you would never have imagined.

"How long'll it take to get to Los Angeles from here?" she said.

"It's about four hundred miles. Maybe four and a half. There's a stretch of desert, the Mohave, we pass by Death Valley. Better to take it after dark. You don't wanta overheat out there."

"I'd just like to get this over with," she said.

"So would I," Wilson said, putting his elbows on the table. "What was the idea?"

"Of what?"

"The whole thing."

She shook her head, almost managed a grin.

"It's going to sound stupid," she said. "It *was* stupid. Okay. We were going to let out the news that I was kidnapped. And I was going to make this video. After a little while we'd send it to the television, and they'd put it on because it'd be news, it'd be showing that I hadn't really been kidnapped and that it was all a trick. And I'd say that they talk about terrorists all the time while they bomb the Palestinian camps and cities in Libya and they torture people in their jails, and the mercenaries they're paying for have killed forty thousand in Nicaragua . . . We'd turn it around on them, see?"

Her face turned red when she had finished, with embarrassment, Wilson supposed, lowering his eyes, glad, for some reason, that she at least realized how silly it sounded. When he looked up again she was blowing smoke at the window.

"So I got this blond wig," she went on dully, after a moment,

117

"and we bought some cheap video equipment and moved into the apartment. I worked very hard on that goddam video. I could recite it for you, but I don't really feel like it."

Wilson leaned against the back of the booth, took a look at the sky. It was clear, pale blue, no clouds, no birds. He shook his head. "I don't get it."

"You don't get it," she repeated hollowly, and shrugged. "It's a lot of things that came together, I guess. Somebody like me—my dad's got lots of money, I'm not bad looking—any way you look at it I'm going to come out a ridiculous person, right? Going to stupid parties and getting my face lifted like my mother. You know what it's like when you can do whatever you want? Nothing you do means anything. I went to work for this stupid newspaper in Denver. I didn't really care about what I was doing there, I just wanted to do something, and I was a joke. Nobody took me seriously. I used to go out with this movie actor for a while. He hasn't gotten famous yet so you haven't heard of him. You see him doing small parts in crummy movies, but I suppose he'll make it big one of these days. I thought he was real neat at first, I liked the way he moved. And then, it took me some time, but eventually I realized that the reason he moved that way was because he thought he was in a movie all the time. He wasn't dumb, but the only thing he ever read was books about Hollywood. The biography of Clark Gable was his favorite."

She shook her head quickly and took a sip of coffee. "Juanjo was the only person I ever met that really cared about things, about anything besides himself. And I suppose, I suppose I wanted to do something real. You get it now?"

"Sure," Wilson said. He wondered if he did.

"Let's get out of this place," she said.

20

The hotel lobby was quiet when Wilson got back, almost no one there and the piped-in music turned down to a funereal whisper. He had the briefcase put back in the hotel safe, and the desk clerk gave him a little printed message form that said that Jilguero had phoned at 22.07 hours and left his number. Wilson sat in the bar for a while, drinking scotch and reading the labels on the bottles behind the bar until his hands stopped shaking. Then he got on the elevator and leaned against the mirror on the back wall and watched the electronic numbers popping up above the door.

The spread was still wrinkled where he had lain on the bed in the afternoon, and a pleasantly familiar trace of the smell of his tobacco was still on the air. He took off his jacket and dropped it on a straight chair, and took the revolver out of his pocket. Sitting on the bed, he snapped out the chamber and took out the three spent shells. Then he put the gun on the bedside table and the shells beside it. He thought about calling Haeflinger and listening to him yell at him, but the prospect of it wasn't very appealing. He lay down and dialed Jilguero's number. It was a little past one-thirty, but he didn't figure Jilguero for the type to go to bed early.

119

Jilguero's voice was tense, flat sounding. "You still ready to pay for information?"

"If it's worth anything," Wilson said. "Is it?"

"I know a guy can maybe tell you something. He just got out of jail a month ago."

Wilson guessed that was supposed to be a kind of recommendation. "So when can I talk to him?"

"Say in an hour?"

"An hour?" Wilson said.

"He needs the money."

"Right," Wilson said resignedly. You can get a lot done if you give up sleeping, he thought. "Where?"

"At the Drugstore on Paseo de Gracia. You know where it is?"

"I'll get a cab," Wilson said. He hung up and lay still on the bed for a moment with his hands folded on his belly and his eyes closed. The electric light on his eyelids kept him awake. Then he got up slowly, put his jacket on, and put the gun in the night-table drawer.

The Drugstore was a big place, an imitation of what the French call a drugstore, which is in turn an imitation of what the French think an American drugstore is, or should be. The result was a lot of glass and aluminum under strong overhead lights. Wilson walked past the boys loitering sulkily, alone or in pairs, on the sidewalk in front of the place, waiting to get picked up, and through the glass doors. People were sitting along an aluminum bar watching something on a television set high up at the far end, the bright lights showing up their bad skin and the red streaks across the whites of their eyes. The place was full of the sound of a girl's voice singing about what sounded like a masochistic relationship with her father. It had a nice tune.

Wilson walked toward the back, past a newsstand, a perfume shop, a place that offered to develop your photos in twenty-four hours, all closed, with metal shutters down in front of them. Jilguero was sitting at a table with a white plastic top, with a bottle of beer in front of him and a little cup of coffee to his right.

"He's in the toilet," Jilguero said. "I think he's got the runs."

"Uh-huh," Wilson said. He ordered a beer and the waiter

brought him a tulip-shaped glass with something like a coat of arms on it with a German name he didn't bother to read. Jilguero avoided his eyes. He didn't look as if he felt like talking.

Jilguero's friend had thick lips and glasses with heavy frames that slid down his nose, a body that seemed to hang on him like a coat a couple of sizes too big. He sat down and put his hands around the empty coffee cup and blinked behind the glasses. They didn't bother with introductions.

"I suppose Jilguero's told you what I want to know?" Wilson said.

"All that," Jilguero's friend said, "is a police setup."

"Yeah?" Wilson said.

"There isn't any anarchist group behind this," the guy said, "or any other group." His voice was pitched a little too high and cracked at the end of his sentences. He looked worn out, and his eyes kept darting from side to side, pointlessly. Maybe that was jail, Wilson thought. He had never been in jail, but he had the idea it probably wasn't very good for your nerves.

"Uh-huh," Wilson said. "How do you know that?"

"I know the people. Besides, nobody's ever done anything at all like this. It's stupid."

Wilson sipped some beer. He was tired, and the music had changed to some kind of disco thing, the sort of mechanical rhythm he was beginning to hate. He wondered if this guy would like the Disneyland idea. He was thinking about trying it on him when the guy started talking again.

"You don't know this country," he said. "The secret police under the dictatorship, they're all still there, they're right at the top, doing the dirty work for the Socialist bureaucrats. I saw the picture of this cop in the newspaper one time—they were making him head of some antiterrorist brigade or something—sitting beside some subsecretary of the Ministry of the Interior, he was the same cop that stuck my head in a toilet back in '73. Who do you think benefits from something like this? Who do you think benefits from all this ETA shit, nowadays? The fascists that wanta keep the apparatus of repression in their hands, right? So who's at the top of the police hierarchy? They're all ex-political police. You check it out. That's how they destroyed the CNT, infiltrating *agents-provocateurs* and

121

backing the most violent, adventurist elements. And that's how they destroyed the revolutionary left in general."

He was red in the face by then, blinking violently. He picked up the empty coffee cup, looked into it, and put it down again sadly. He had a timid, sad kind of look on his face when he wasn't talking, worn out.

Wilson rubbed his eyes. "Look," he said. "I didn't really come down here for a lesson in political science, you know?"

The guy just looked a little sadder. Jilguero tilted back his chair, looking at Wilson, and managed a mild sneer around the cigarette in his mouth. His hair was growing out. It looked like a couple of days' growth of beard all over the top of his head. He was wearing a faded green sleeveless T-shirt and baggy trousers, and people stared at him as they passed, even in the Drugstore where there was no shortage of strange-looking people.

"Let's get to the point," Wilson said.

Jilguero's friend looked at the table. "Jilguero says you're looking for somebody," he said slowly, "somebody named Juanjo."

"Yeah," Wilson said. "You know him?"

"I've known people named Juanjo. What's he got to do with it?"

"Maybe nothing. I don't know."

The guy with the glasses looked at him sourly. "So?"

"He was involved with the girl, just before she disappeared. So he's a lead, the sort of thing you gotta check out. Doesn't mean anything to start with. Or maybe it does. You wanta look at the money first, or what?"

"What's he look like?"

"Dark hair. Medium height, medium build, pretty medium as far as I can gather."

"I knew a guy like that," Jilguero's friend said, blinking.

He needs the money, Wilson thought. It would be pretty easy to take a guy like me for a ride. Not being the suspicious type. It being three o'clock in the morning after kind of a rough night. "Anything special about him?"

Jilguero's friend wrinkled his forehead, put the tip of his finger to his chin, and said, "I think he had a sort of hole here, like Cary Grant."

122

"I heard Kirk Douglas," Wilson said. "I guess that's close enough."

Jilguero's friend nodded sadly. Jilguero put his mouth over the top of the bottle and leaned his head back.

"It's what I was telling you," Jilguero's friend said.

"What do you mean?"

Jilguero's friend wiped his lips with the back of his hand. "He used to be a friend of mine," he said quietly with his eyes on the table, fiddling with the handle of the coffee cup. "We were in the same group. It doesn't matter what we were doing. Juanjo was a good talker—and that was mostly what we did—maybe too good, maybe he got carried away with the sound of his own voice sometimes. This was in 1976, '77. Eventually everybody in the group got busted, everybody except Juanjo. That didn't mean anything, could have been coincidence, but then when I got out I found out he'd been in a couple of other groups and more or less the same thing had happened. And there were things the cops knew about our operations, it seemed like they must have got the information from the inside. People were starting to talk by then. Juanjo wasn't around when I got out. He just wasn't around, and we'd been good friends. I guess he had his reasons for not wanting to see me."

Wilson drank some of his beer and began mechanically filling his pipe. He was tired, and the beer was making him sleepy, slightly muddled.

"What you mean to say, exactly . . . ?"

"He was working for the cops," Jilguero's friend said quickly, his voice rising to a kind of squeak. "He was working for the cops then, maybe he's working for them now."

"You seen him since?"

"No."

Wilson lit his pipe, shook the match out, and dropped it on the floor. He puffed a little and blew out little clouds of smoke. "That'd be like ten, eleven, years ago, right? What's he been doing all this time?"

Jilguero's friend shrugged and looked a little sadder. "I think somebody told me once he met him on the street. Said he was going to the university."

* * *

123

It was a funny, confused sort of dream, and when he woke up he had the feeling that he had probably missed the point. It was still dark on the other side of the curtains, the room was heavy with a thick humming darkness. He was wondering about the dream when he realized that the telephone was ringing and had been ringing for some time. As he fumbled for the receiver it occurred to him that if it hadn't been for the telephone he would never have thought of the dream, it would have been just as if it had never happened.

The voice on the telephone said it belonged to somebody named Valcarca, and Wilson tried to think who that was. His eyes were getting used to the darkness, he could make out and recognize the shapes of the furniture. It gave him an odd, empty feeling, as if he had lost something.

"They say they know where she is," Valcarca's voice said, sounding clipped and excited. "The tactical squad's going in. Television's going to be there. I thought you'd like to know."

"Yeah," Wilson said. He drank some water from the glass on the night table. The luminous dial on his travel clock read five past five. "Thanks."

"Wilson?"

"Yeah?" Wilson said. He had gone back to sleep again, for just a moment. "Where?"

Valcarca gave him the address and Wilson wrote it down on the little pad the hotel had put beside the phone with its monogram on the top of each sheet. The light hurt his eyes when he switched it on.

"I'm on my way down there now," Valcarca said. Wilson thanked him again and hung up. He lay his head down on the pillow and closed his eyes for a second while electric colors spun around behind his eyelids. Then he pulled the covers off and swung around into a sitting position. His body felt slack and clumsy.

He put his head under the cold-water tap and bumped it coming up. He brushed his teeth, dressed, and poured a couple of fingers of whiskey into the water glass. He gagged when he drank it, then stood there taking deep breaths, eyes watering, and managed to keep it down.

There was no sound but the faint unearthly hum of the air-conditioning in the corridor, but music was still whispering in the elevator Wilson took down to the street floor. The lobby was fully

124

lit, empty except for a woman in a blue smock vacuuming the carpet and the man behind the desk who looked up at Wilson over the top of his book. Wilson gave him his key and went out the sliding glass doors to the street.

The sky was a murky dark, starless. A few cars flashed by at high speeds, taking advantage of the empty streets, last survivors of the night with blaring radios and a sprinkling of early risers. Wilson stood on the curb waiting for a cab to come by. There was no wind in the trees. It felt as if it were going to be hot again.

The taxi smelled of hashish, even with the window open. The driver had pimples on the back of his neck and drove as if he thought he was a fighter pilot, cutting across the empty lanes with a demented little smile on his face while the neon colors flashed across the windshield. Wilson saw the statue of Columbus on a pillar hurtling toward them through half-lit space, wondered for a moment if they were going to make it, and dozed off to the hum of the engine.

When he opened his eyes again the light was coming up, thin and powdery. There were big trees overhanging an open paved area at the center of an avenue, parked cars and shuttered shops at the bottom of gray-faced, sleeping buildings. The cab turned in, then slowed abruptly when the driver saw the police van.

"What's going on?" he said.

"Nothing," Wilson said.

A uniformed policeman looked him over as he got out of the taxi and then lost interest. There were a number of people, all standing around rather pointlessly in the dawning light, policemen with their trousers tucked into the tops of their boots and bright-yellow foulards. The television van had a mass of thick black cable dumped out of the side door like spilled entrails on the pavement. They were all looking up a narrow street that came off the avenue, not much wider than an alley. There were two cops standing at the beginning of the street, looking proprietary. The buildings were old around there, with a crumbly look to them.

"You're too late," Valcarca said irritably, fumbling a cigarette pack out of his shoulder bag. "So was I."

"What's going on?" Wilson said.

"They already went in," Valcarca said, lighting his cigarette

125

and then looking at his watch. "Ten minutes ago now. They let the TV people through, I asked the cop over there how come they let the TV people through and not the rest of us. He said he didn't know, but maybe it was because a lot of people that watch television can't read."

Valcarca shook his head disgustedly, shifted the bag on his shoulder, and peered down the narrow street, where nothing at all appeared to be happening. Daylight was just beginning to seep down there between the high walls, and the streetlights were still on. A skinny brown dog slunk past the cops with a piece of bloody butcher paper in his mouth, glancing warily up at them as if he expected a kick, and scurried off at a trot.

A bum was sitting behind them on a stone bench covered with newspapers, hunched forward and watching them with a muddled, malevolent glare. Cops probably woke him up, Wilson thought. He had a deep tan, hard like varnished wood, a black beard streaked with gray.

"I talked to a guy," Wilson said, "said it was all a police setup."

"An anarchist, right?" Valcarca snorted, with a little smile. "Anarchists think everything's a police setup."

He was watching a man coming down the street toward them with a heavy-looking video camera on his shoulder. He passed the cops at the end of the street, Valcarca and the other reporters swarmed around him.

"They changed their minds," the cameraman said, lowering the camera off his shoulder. "They won't let us in the building now. A couple of plainclothes cops went in."

More police cars arrived, with blue lights spinning on top, men got out with heavy-looking cases and went up the street. The bum was gone when Wilson looked around again and had taken the newspapers with him. Wilson walked over and sat down on the bench. It looked like it was going to take awhile. The same dog trotted by again, looking worried. It was the sort of dog that always looked worried. A few people passing by stopped to gawk for a moment and then went on. Wilson started filling his pipe, wondering if a beer would take away the nasty taste in his mouth. The light was beginning to hurt his eyes.

126

There was a flurry of movement, Valcarca and the other people crowded around somebody Wilson couldn't see. He thought about getting up and decided not to bother. The group broke up, and Valcarca came over with a crooked little half-repressed grin on his face and sat down beside him on the bench.

"They found a body, apparently," he said.

Wilson held a breath, kept on tamping down the tobacco automatically with his thumb. He didn't know the girl, he was too sleepy really to care very much.

"Was it her?"

Valcarca shook his head. "No, some guy. They're not saying anything yet. The cops are pissed off at the TV guys, because they think they're going to make them come out looking silly, I suppose, and the TV guys are pissed off at the cops because they didn't keep their agreement to let them film inside."

"And the dead guy's probably pissed off because he's dead," Wilson said. "What about the girl?"

"Apparently she's not there."

"You wanta get some coffee?"

"No, they'll have to make some kind of statement pretty soon," Valcarca said. He stood up wearily and walked back to where the TV people and the other reporters were standing around. Wilson rested his forearms on his legs and looked at the pavement around his feet. When he looked up the reporters were forming a tight circle around someone and Zapatero shouldered his way through it, leaving the other cop to do the talking, Wilson thought. He stood up, wondering if Zapatero would come to him or if he would have to go after him.

Zapatero didn't look happy to see him, he didn't look happy about anything. His skin had a gray, sickly tone in the sunshine, bloodshot eyes blinking sadly.

"You're up early, Mr. Wilson," he said.

"Who's the stiff?"

"Gentleman named Juan José Silvestre."

"Juanjo," Wilson said.

"Name sound familiar?"

"I talked to a guy, he said Juanjo used to work for you people."

Zapatero glanced away down the street, scowling. The televi-

127

sion technicians were stowing their gear in the van, the street was beginning to wake up, with the groan of shutters opening, car engines starting up. Zapatero took out a pair of sunglasses and put them on.

"I talk to people every day who tell me stupid things," he said. "You get used to it."

"You could check it out."

"I could."

"What about the girl?"

"She was there. There's a woman's stuff in the bathroom."

"How did you know she was there?"

"We got a tip," Zapatero mumbled.

"You got any idea where she is now?"

"Would I tell you if I did? You're a tourist. I don't usually talk to tourists. I'm wondering why I'm making an exception in your case. What do you know, Wilson?"

Wilson knocked the ashes out of his pipe and put it in his pocket. "The same thing you do, I suppose, that Juanjo was her boyfriend. Doesn't make much sense, does it?"

"No?" Zapatero said, with a sour twist to the corner of his mouth. "You still think things are supposed to make sense, Wilson? This is the twentieth century."

2 1

"It was Silvestre that rented the apartment," Valcarca said. "The neighbors say he was with a blond woman. The cops found a blond wig in the apartment. It's all fitting together. They had the right place, they were just a little late."

Valcarca sounded enthusiastic again. Wilson lay on the bed with the phone to his ear, watching the pattern on the wallpaper jiggle like a mirage.

"They said he was shot around twelve," Valcarca went on. "They didn't find the gun in the apartment. One of the neighbors thinks she remembers hearing the shot. She thought it was something on the television."

The light was changing outside the window. It was going to be dark in not too long. Wilson had slept for a few hours that morning, woke up about noon with a hangover and the feeling that nothing he could do was going to make the least bit of difference. The cafeteria had a fountain in the middle that looked like an oversize aluminum dildo with colored lights on it. He spent quite awhile sitting there drinking coffee and then went up to his room and spent the afternoon telephoning people that weren't there. Haeflinger, when he finally got on to him, yelled for awhile as usual and then said he would call him back. Schumacher was out of the office most of the day, and when he finally came on the line he sounded as if he had been having a nap. Wilson told him what had happened, but he didn't sound very interested.

"This guy started shooting at me," Wilson said, knowing there wasn't any point. It felt like swimming through mud. "I didn't like that. I get nervous when people shoot at me."

"I'm sorry about that, Mr. Wilson," Schumacher said sleepily. "I hope you've still got the money, haven't you?"

"Who set up the exchange?" Wilson said. "Who was it that talked to you people?"

"Oh, I couldn't tell you that, Mr. Wilson," Schumacher said.

So Wilson had called Valcarca's newspaper three or four times, and now he was holding the phone to his ear listening to Valcarca, watching the reflections slide like liquid over the windows, the twilight making sad shadows across the room. The place was beginning to scare him, for no particular reason, just too much coffee and not enough sleep.

"Look," he said, cutting Valcarca off in midsentence, "put in your article that the stiff was a police informer—according to informed sources, or whatever it is you guys say. I'm an informed source, right?"

Valcarca mumbled something hesitantly. "What's the idea?"

"I don't know," Wilson said, closing his eyes, sliding down on the bed so that his head was flat on the pillow. "Just fucking put it in, all right? It's a good angle, isn't it?"

"Is it?" Valcarca said. "Why?"

"It'd explain why they killed him, wouldn't it?"

Wilson ate a dull supper in the hotel restaurant, a shrimp salad in a pink sauce and a tasteless rabbit in a salty brown sauce, and drank a half bottle of overpriced red wine. He went back up to his room and read a couple of chapters more of Gibbon's *Decline and Fall* in which the Byzantine Empire held on hundreds of years longer than it seemed it should have out of sheer inertia, bureaucratic slyness, or perhaps just a genius for accumulating enough cash to

130

buy off successive waves of threatening barbarians. When the telephone rang it was Haeflinger again.

"She just walked onto a goddam airplane," he snarled, "and walked right off again in New York. So you better get your ass over here."

The girl at the travel desk in the hotel got him a reservation on a flight to New York leaving early that afternoon. Wilson packed his things, put the gun back in its box, and told the desk clerk to send it to Schumacher by messenger. Then he took the briefcase with the money in it out of the hotel safe and took it back to the bank. The streets, already steaming in the morning heat, with café tables on the sidewalks and the deep green leaves on the trees, looked almost pretty out the taxi window. A lot of places begin to look better just when you're leaving, Wilson thought.

When he got back to the hotel he paid the bill at the desk with his Visa card and then took the elevator up to the Moonlight Room at the top. He had been curious about the Moonlight Room when he checked in, but he hadn't gotten around to visiting it, and he had a couple of hours before he needed to leave for the airport.

It was like a sort of penthouse, built facing the sea, with the back wall covered by one immense mural, palm trees and a tropical beach in washed out pastel colors. What sounded like '50s dance music was coming out of speakers in the corners, and there was nobody there but a waiter polishing glasses behind a long bar and two people standing out on the terrace on the other side of the glass front. Outside the sky was a bright blue, and below it a dirty haze hovered over endless buildings that seemed to crumble indistinguishably into one another while occasional giants of steel and glass rose up out of the midst of them like sinister towers. The city scooped downward to the sea, and there were freighters lying up offshore and a long curve of concrete breakwater cut out into the blue-green water. The people on the terrace were a middle-age Japanese couple. The man had longish dark hair streaked with gray. He was resting his elbows on the ledge at the edge of the terrace, taking pictures with a camera with a telephoto lens. Wilson sat down and leaned his head back. The sun on his face felt good.

The waiter had a wispy mustache and a sullen manner, as if he wanted to make it clear that he resented having been exiled up there to sweep up bird droppings and take in small tips.

"Have you got champagne?" Wilson asked him.

"Yes, sir," the waiter said. "A half bottle?"

"No, a regular bottle. Very dry, very cold, very expensive."

The waiter gave him a funny look and went off to look for an ice bucket. When he came back with it he pulled over another small table and put the bucket on it. Then he brought out the bottle and popped the cork and poured out a glass and stood there looking sarcastic until Wilson had tried the champagne and said it was all right. Then the waiter put the bottle in the metal bucket, draped a linen towel over its shoulders, and went away.

The glass was tall and narrow, with a thin stem, and the champagne had an icy, smoothly dry taste, like something you could drink a lot of, floating off on the bubbles. Wilson didn't guess it would matter, there wasn't anything left that he had to do, except get on an airplane.

"Is it your birthday, Wilson?"

Wilson looked up and saw Zapatero standing there, throwing a shadow across his table, a blotch of gray surrounded by a pale glare, gray suit with the jacket unbuttoned, dark glasses.

Zapatero dropped a four-by-four photograph on the table. Wilson picked it up by one corner and squinted at it. Head and shoulders of a man with dark hair and a strong nose. The eyes were wide open and looked very tired. It seemed like a picture of somebody that had died a long time ago, in some war that everybody's forgotten about.

"They found him yesterday," Zapatero said, "in a ditch with a lot of other garbage."

"Who?" Wilson said quietly.

"Somebody's dog," Zapatero said. He pulled back the chair on the other side of the table and the metal legs scraped on the tiles. "You know him?"

Wilson didn't say anything. He was thinking about going to jail, wondering if Haeflinger would be able to get him out, or if he would try. So he didn't say anything. Zapatero didn't seem to mind.

"I was reading this report," he said, putting his cigarettes on the table, "about an incident the other night in front of a place

132

called the Best Pig Pub. Between an Arabic gentleman and a fat man with an American accent. It said some shots were fired. The fat American sounded a lot like you."

"What is it you want?" Wilson said.

Zapatero smiled faintly, just turning up the corners of his mouth below the dark lenses. Wilson didn't like the smile, he didn't like not being able to see his eyes. He could feel the sweat sliding down out of his armpits. These guys like making people scared, he thought. It's what they do best.

"They told me downstairs that you were checking out, going back to the United States this afternoon. I thought I'd like to get this thing cleared up with you."

"The girl's gone," Wilson said, "back to the States."

"That's nice for her," Zapatero said. He didn't seem very surprised. "So you paid them off?"

"No," Wilson said. Zapatero would know that, or should have. "She just walked on the plane, using her own passport. It seems a little too easy, doesn't it?"

Zapatero shrugged. Wilson reached slowly for the champagne glass and took a sip. It still tasted good, strangely enough.

"What about the Arab?" Zapatero said.

Wilson shook his head, turning the stem of the champagne glass between his fingers.

"It'd be better for you to cooperate," Zapatero said. It was the sort of thing cops said and just let the implications hang there, like nightmares you could read between the lines in daily newspapers.

"Not unless I know where I am," Wilson said. "Are you charging me with something?"

"I could," Zapatero said, taking a cigarette out of the pack and picking up his lighter. He was taking his time, enjoying it. "The Arab died of a shot of heroin that had too much strychnine in the cut. Happens all the time. He had a couple of marks on his arm, but they'd been made at the same time. The guy who did the autopsy thought that was kind of funny. That and the bullet in his leg. But it's not much, maybe they won't even call it homicide. And it doesn't really sound to me like your style, Mr. Wilson. It's not my case anyway. I just happened to read the report. You learn things sometimes, reading the reports."

133

"Have you got anything on him?"

Zapatero shook his head and pointed a finger at Wilson. "It's your turn now."

Wilson lifted the champagne bottle out of the bucket, let it drip for a moment before wrapping the towel around it and pouring it into his glass. "You want some champagne?"

"I'd rather have whiskey," Zapatero said. He waved a finger at the waiter and ordered a Ballantine's.

"I was supposed to give the Arab the money when the girl was delivered," Wilson said. "She didn't show up, and he tried to take the money anyway."

"So you shot him?"

"In the leg."

The waiter put a tall glass in front of Zapatero, poured the whiskey over the ice, and tipped up the bottle with a flourish.

"You got the money back?"

Wilson nodded.

"Who arranged for the exchange?"

"I don't know," Wilson said. "Ask Schumacher."

"Schumacher's just an aged messenger boy," Zapatero said contemptuously.

Messenger boy, Wilson thought. The champagne was still cold, the bubbles tickled the inside of his nose. Like me, he thought. And what do you think you are?

"It was set up through the consulate," Wilson said. "Maybe those guys know what's going on. Why don't you ask 'em?"

Zapatero drank some whiskey and the lines in his forehead converged in a frown.

"Who was he?" Wilson said. "The Arab?"

"Small-time crook. He's served time in France and here. He's been a pimp, small-time dope dealer."

"Nothing political?"

"No."

The Japanese couple were sitting a few tables away with small glasses of fruit juice in front of them. The man was taking apart his camera, studying the parts with seemingly fanatical intensity while the woman stared patiently off into the smog. Wilson drank some champagne.

"Was Juanjo working for you people?" he said.

"I seem to remember you asking me that before, Mr. Wilson," Zapatero said tiredly. "We don't keep files on informers."

"I thought you guys kept files on everything," Wilson said. "Anyway, somebody would know."

"Maybe," Zapatero said with his eyes half closed. "Who told you all that?"

Wilson shook his head, with a little conciliatory smile. "I couldn't tell you that," he said. "I'm getting on a plane in an hour. This isn't my problem. And I don't think you really want to know anyway, do you?"

Wilson stopped there, and waited. Don't make him mad, he thought. Zapatero sat slumped in his chair, with wrinkles in his suit and sweat stains on his shirt collar. He just looked like an old guy in a rumpled suit, but you didn't want to make him mad. And the trouble was that these guys liked to get mad.

"Why is that?" Zapatero said mildly.

Wilson took a sip of champagne. He was beginning to feel it. Perhaps he had been feeling it for a while without noticing. It occurred to him that maybe he would be better off shutting up.

"I mean," he said slowly, "that the Arab's dead and Juanjo's dead, the girl's gone back to the States, and I'm going. That's everybody I know of that knows anything about this thing, out of the way. It'd be pretty hard for whoever's behind this to have it all work out that well. Without any help, I mean."

Zapatero kept on smiling at the corners of his mouth. "That's very pretty, Wilson," he said. "You don't believe in coincidences?"

"Sometimes," Wilson said. The Japanese couple were gathering up their camera equipment and guide books and maps and putting them in nylon carrier bags, talking together in Japanese words, in short sentences that sounded brusque and hurried. "Who sent the GEOs, the tactical squad, in?"

"It didn't go through us."

"But you could find out."

"Maybe."

"Or maybe you don't really want to."

Zapatero leaned back and the metal chair creaked faintly. "It's not quite as simple as that," he said with a certain exaggerated

135

patience. He put another cigarette in his mouth and watched the Japanese couple walking across the empty barroom to the elevator.

"What I'm not quite clear about," Wilson said, "is why you're sitting here talking to me."

"I'm working," Zapatero said, drinking some whiskey. "There are other services in on this investigation. We don't always talk to one another very much. So maybe what I find out somebody else has already known for quite a while. I bring in a few pieces. Somebody else puts them together. You think you've got it all figured out, Wilson?"

"I'm guessing," Wilson said. "I'm a pretty good guesser."

"Go on."

"There wasn't anybody in this but Juanjo, was there?"

"No?"

"Juanjo and one other guy, the guy that was running him. No organization, I mean. That was just a front, a fake."

"What about the Arab?"

"The Arab was a messenger boy. Like me."

"And the other guy?"

"He was a cop."

Zapatero didn't flinch. He just looked bored, with the black lenses in front of his eyes, and rattled the ice in his glass.

"Stop me if I'm telling you what you already know," Wilson said.

"I don't know anything," Zapatero said dryly. "But I think maybe I heard this before."

"Juanjo was an informer," Wilson said. "Check it out. Maybe there's no way to check it out. Ten years ago. Okay. But the guys that were running him then, let's suppose they're still around. So how come they don't say anything when you come up with his body. Huh? It's no big deal. A lot of informers are crooks, that's why they're informers. But nobody says anything. You follow me?"

Zapatero put his chin in his hand. Maybe the heat was making him tired. Wilson poured out the last of the champagne. Stoned, he thought, and the sun dazzled his eyes. He was getting lost, it was all words anyway, and maybe in the end the son of a bitch was going to take him in, stick him in a concrete cell, and he'd go through the same thing under bright milky-white lights.

"I gotta catch a plane," he said.

136

"You got time," Zapatero said. "How come they let the girl walk away?"

"Maybe Juanjo got cold feet," Wilson said. "Lies are cheap, you know. Maybe when you're making your living with lies you get kind of confused yourself. I don't know."

He looked at the black lenses on Zapatero's sunglasses. Reflections of sunlight splashed across them, shifted when he lowered his head.

"So the cop blew his brains out. Two hundred thousand dollars, it's enough to piss somebody off when he's counting on it. Or maybe he was figuring on doing it in the first place."

"Yeah?" Zapatero said. Wilson drank the rest of his champagne. It wasn't very cold anymore, and had a kind of sticky taste.

"He wouldn't have sent the GEOs in if he thought he was in there alive, would he?"

"It's good," Zapatero said, blowing out some smoke, "but it's not that good."

"No?" Wilson said. "I don't really give a shit. I gotta catch a plane. You knew all that anyway, you just maybe didn't want to think about it."

"Going after another cop's a messy business," Zapatero said, "and maybe nobody'll thank you for it. I put in my reports, somebody else'll figure it out. In this country everything is politics, you know. In America, you haven't got any politics, you've just got guns."

"Sure," Wilson said, stuffing tobacco into his pipe. It didn't make any difference anymore. They were just a couple of old guys being tough with one another.

"You see the paper this morning?"

"No," Wilson said. He couldn't really remember.

"The ETA blew up another car bomb in Zaragoza. Three people dead, I think. No policeman this time." Zapatero drank the rest of his whiskey, watered with the melted ice, and made a face.

"So I don't think anybody's going to be very interested in this thing here. It hasn't come out too bad. There's one Arab dead—nobody gives that much of a damn about another dead Arab. One dead terrorist. The stupid little girl's gone back to where she came from."

137

"I've gotta get going," Wilson said, lighting his pipe.

"Just one thing," Zapatero said. "I'd just like to tell you one thing, just as a favor."

Wilson looked at him, not liking the sound of it. He didn't think he wanted any favors from Zapatero.

"We found a videotape in the flat. The girl was on it, making a speech in her pidgin Spanish. She said she hadn't been kidnapped. She said she'd been in on it from the beginning, that it was some kind of revolutionary plot to get on television."

Wilson nodded sleepily and looked out across the city to the place where the sea seemed to melt into the sky. There seemed to be a kind of line, but when you looked closely you saw that you had only imagined it there.

"I think they gave the tape to your friends at the consulate," Zapatero said. "Have a nice journey, Wilson."

2 2

It was getting dark by the time they got to the California border. A tall cop wearing high-heeled boots and a frontier .45 on his hip stepped off the porch of a little white stucco building with CALIFOR-NIA STATE POLICE written over the door and took his time walking over to the car, swaying a little, as if he had just gotten off a horse.

Wilson didn't see anyone else around, though there could have been another cop or two in the building. The car parked alongside had lots of different-colored lights on it and looked like it would go pretty fast. The sky above the tiled roof was orange, while the rest of it was turning from deep blue to black. Wilson rolled down the window and didn't bother trying to smile.

The cop leaned close to the window and glanced over the inside of the car, winced when he sniffed the stale beer smell coming off it, and then grinned slyly at Wilson when he had looked Elizabeth over. He asked Wilson if they were carrying any fresh fruits, vegeta-bles, or flowering plants, and Wilson said they weren't. The cop straightened up and waved them through. Wilson put his foot down on the gas and they started across California. It looked like the same black strip of endless highway.

"He just came in that day," Elizabeth said, picking it up again, as if she didn't realize she hadn't said anything for half an hour, staring straight out the bug-smeared windshield, talking to herself or to the dark, as if Wilson weren't really there at all. "All of a sudden. I was watching television, I guess. He said to come on, he said the plan was changed, we were going to take a ransom. I didn't know what he was talking about. He wasn't acting like he usually did. He was trying to sound hard. He wasn't like that, he was gentle. I just said no. The television was going and he got mad and started yelling at me. He said all that we'd talked about was all bullshit. It was just words, he said, the only thing that's real is money."

She stopped then and Wilson heard something like the sound of a dry chuckle. "Just like my parents have been telling me all my life, you know? The same old shit."

Sure, Wilson thought, they always tell you that.

"I just kept saying no, and then he started, like he was going to cry. He said it would just be for a little while, we'd get the money and then we could be together again, we'd be free, we could go wherever we wanted. We could go to Martinique, he said, I don't know why he thought I wanted to go to Martinique. I just said no. I said a bunch of other things I guess, I don't remember, and then he started coming toward me, like he didn't have time to fool around any more. Maybe he said that, I don't know. And I took the gun out of the drawer and pointed it at him, and he started laughing, this ugly, hysterical kind of laugh, like I was just this stupid bitch, and he was getting closer. And then I guess he made a move, I guess, and I shot him."

"Shit," Wilson said softly.

"It was easy, you know?" she said, as if that still surprised her.

Wilson guessed she was crying then, soundlessly, with her head down in the dark. A billboard went past, with some kids on it drinking 7-Up.

"Juanjo was working for the cops," Wilson said after a while, "or a cop. Selling 'em information about an organization that didn't exist. But when they found out that your old man had money they decided to go for the ransom. Juanjo and the cop. I don't know quite how it worked out, but that's the gist of it."

"I don't believe that," Elizabeth said quietly.

140

"Yeah. Well, it doesn't make any difference to me."

She turned on the radio after a while, and the man said tomorrow was going to be just as hot as it had been today. He sounded pleased about it. There was a town every twenty minutes or so. They were all just about the same, with a burst of light around the drive-in hamburger places and then the long, dim-lit main street with shops with big dark show windows looking out on empty sidewalks. Wilson remembered living in a town like that when he was just out of high school, how they used to drive like mad down dark highways like that one just to listen to a jukebox in some roadside café or sit drinking beer on somebody's front porch. There was a road up into the mountains and they would go up there sometimes, drunk usually, and look down on everything, the lights blinking off in distance where you could see the cars moving along the highway and other mountains way off. He could hardly remember now. The night roads had felt different then. It was a long time ago.

They could have been behind him for quite a while before he realized they were there, almost all the way from the border maybe, the lights in his rearview mirror keeping their distance. That was what started him thinking in the first place, the way they kept their distance, and then he glimpsed the shape of the Dodge in the mirror sliding under gas station lights. He hit the gas and saw the speedometer gauge flicker, then let up. The headlights didn't seem to be coming any closer. They were hanging back there, waiting for him to stop maybe. The radio was playing soft country-western, mostly about getting straight with the Lord. He didn't like having to keep watching the rearview mirror. They probably knew that, he thought. It was probably part of the game.

Elizabeth was sleeping, her head tilted against the window. A neon marquee in front of a cocktail lounge in the middle of nowhere said LAST WATERHOLE THIS SIDE OF DEATH VALLEY. TOPLESS. Wilson started taking up the speed gradually, knowing it wouldn't do any good, just to do something.

The next town they hit was the sort of place nobody outside of a fifty-mile radius had ever heard of, but there was still some action on Main Street, kids driving up and down in pickups and old cars that they revved hard at the stoplights or Porsches their daddies had given them for managing to graduate from high school. Wilson

141

slipped into the lineup at the traffic lights, took the cross street and kept on turning for a while. The streets were lined with rickety-looking bungalows with the soft glow of television screens on picture window curtains.

"Where you going?" Elizabeth said sleepily. She straightened up and pushed back her hair with her fingers and looked dazedly around her. "Where's this?"

"I gotta piss," Wilson said. It sounded like a pretty good reason, and besides it was true.

"Me too," Elizabeth said.

They found a gas station eventually, on the other side of a used car lot under sickly yellow lights. Wilson told the kid to fill it up and they walked around the side of the building to the toilets. When Elizabeth went into the Ladies, Wilson walked back around to the front of the station, went inside, and put some coins into the telephone on the wall. Haeflinger was at home. Wilson could hear the sound of the television behind him, rifle shots and melodramatic music.

"Where the hell have you been?" Haeflinger said.

"I been trying to find Elizabeth Dantry, remember? Well, I found her."

"Where are you?"

"In California. There's a couple of guys following us in a Dodge. You know what they want?"

Haeflinger didn't say anything for a minute. Wilson looked out the window at the kid poking at things under the hood of the car and hoped Elizabeth would take her time.

"Dantry wants her out of the country," Haeflinger said. He sounded embarrassed, and it took a lot to embarrass Haeflinger.

"What's that supposed to mean?"

"The boyfriend, the stiff in the apartment, it seems like he went over to the Libyan Embassy, tried to sell 'em something they didn't want, and somebody took his picture. And then there's this video. You know about the video?"

"Yeah."

"You could've fucking told me about it."

"I've been busy," Wilson said.

"Well, those guys want to talk to her about that, and Dantry

142

wants her out of here. He doesn't want all this shit to get out. He figures she goes away they'll just forget about it."

Wilson watched the kid hanging up the gas hose, standing there with the moths fluttering around him, scratching his armpit. "What do you want me to do?"

"You dodge those guys, you get her on an airplane to Guatemala or Brazil or any of those fucking places, I don't care. Dantry doesn't care either."

"What if she doesn't want to go?"

"You're a tough guy, right, Wilson? You're a veteran and all that. You get her little ass on the airplane. Is she nuts?"

"No," Wilson said. "She's not nuts."

"Where are you in California?"

"A little east of San Bernardino, I guess."

"Okay, you get her to the Los Angeles Airport tomorrow morning. Say seven or eight o'clock. Ask for a ticket in her name at the Pan Am desk. Tell her he'll send her money to American Express wherever the fuck it is she's going. Tell her she's still got her meal ticket."

She was standing there then, under the floodlights, looking at him through the big window over the tops of the oil cans.

"But if those guys get close to you," Haeflinger ground on, "you put your thumb up your ass and act like you got no idea what the hell's goin' on. I don't want any trouble with those guys, understand?"

"Sure," Wilson said. He hung up the phone and went outside. It was still hot, and the air smelled of gas. She was leaning against the car door, and the gas station kid was standing a little to one side, scratching himself and trying to look indifferent.

"You always take the keys, don't you?" she said.

"Conditioned reflex," Wilson said.

"I was beginning to think I could trust you."

"I had to call my boss," Wilson said, paying the kid. "I work for a living, you know?"

He got into the car and she got in on the other side.

"Your old man wants to buy you a ticket to South America," he said. For a second she looked as if she were going to say some-

143

thing, but she didn't. Wilson put the key in the ignition and started the car.

The Dodge passed them going the other way, tried a fast U-turn that didn't work and had to back up. Wilson took the first left, guessing, and sped down an empty street lined with sad, droopy trees, then turned again. He heard a dog bark somewhere and out of the corner of his eyes he saw Elizabeth take the automatic out of her purse and twist around in the seat.

"What the hell do you think you're going to do with that?" he said.

"I don't know," she said, watching the back window.

Wilson kept on taking the turns, moving fast but trying not to let the tires squeal. They were on the edge of town again, vacant lots and trailer houses and an old walled graveyard.

Wilson drove into a back alley with an empty field on his left, cut the lights, and slammed on the brake. When Elizabeth lurched forward he caught her wrist with one hand and twisted it and grabbed the gun with the other. He tossed it out the open window and heard it plop heavily into the weeds. The crickets stopped chirping for a minute.

"You get a kick out of this or something?" he said.

"I guess I knew you could do that if you wanted to," she said. She was holding onto her wrist, but it didn't look like it hurt very much.

"Shit," Wilson said. He opened the car door and got out and stood there in the road. He didn't have any idea why he was standing in the road, but he didn't feel like doing anything else. There was another dog barking, or maybe it was the same dog. He could smell the weeds and somebody's chili con carne supper. She got out and walked around the front of the car. Wilson wondered what he would do if the guys in the Dodge came down the alley just then.

"Look," he said, "I'll get you out of this, all right? That's what you want, isn't it?"

"What do you want?"

Wilson looked at her for a moment, and when her eyes didn't panic he leaned closer and kissed her. She put her palms on his chest, and Wilson forgot that he was a fat man.

144

"That was nice," she said afterward. "But it doesn't solve anything, does it?"

It's a long time coming into Los Angeles. Wilson held onto the wheel and read the names of towns that went by on the signs over the freeway and tried to keep off the tiredness and the panic. The sneaking fear that things could just go on like that, forever, rows of red brake lights blinking off and on in the traffic jams and the ambulances screaming by along the access lanes. At least he didn't have to worry about anybody finding them there. He couldn't even have found himself.

They hadn't seen the Dodge behind them since the town where they stopped. That should have seemed strange, but Wilson was too tired to think about it. He was shaking by then, he could see his hand shake when he switched the station on the radio. There were plenty to choose from then, fifty or so stations with fast-talking disc jockeys who all sounded as if they were on amphetamines. Kids dragged Main Street twenty-four hours a day there, even after they stopped being kids, and it was all Main Street.

The airport parking lot was the size of a small town. Wilson took a time ticket out of a machine and parked, and they walked to the terminal building, watching a big plane climbing up in the dark sky behind it, with lights twinkling on its nose and the tips of the wings.

They picked up her ticket at the Pan American desk, one way to Rio de Janeiro. It was still dark then, and the airport was quiet, with cleaners pushing their wide dusters across the shiny floor. They stood in line and checked Elizabeth's suitcase. The flight left in about two hours.

"He wants me as far away as he can get me, doesn't he?" Elizabeth said.

They had bacon and eggs and coffee in a place called the Cloud Room, watching big planes jockeying around on the runways like awkward birds and not saying much to one another. The bacon was cut thin and cooked so dry it crumbled, but the eggs were good, and Wilson enjoyed dunking his toast in the yellow. It had started getting light then, and it was pretty watching the color of the sky change. They drank more coffee, and Elizabeth paged through the

145

pile of magazines she had bought for the trip and Wilson smoked and felt lousy.

After a while they went downstairs and found the international flight departure lounge. Wilson thought about kissing her again, but there didn't seem to be any point. Then he began to feel silly standing there thinking about it and just said good-bye. He watched her go through the ticket check and on past a glass wall, and when she didn't turn around he walked back across the terminal and out the front door. He was thinking about getting a motel room and sleeping for a couple of days, maybe getting a couple of six-packs of beer and watching television for a while to relax first, figuring out his hours and calling Haeflinger to tell him how much overtime he owed him.

The Dodge was almost right in front of him when he came out the door, in an emergency no-parking zone, with an airport cop standing over it to make sure they didn't tow it away. Wilson turned fast and the automatic double doors swished open again.

Haeflinger, he thought, because that was the only way it made sense. Haeflinger playing it safe, playing it both ways. Collect from Dantry and keep in good with the cops too. It sounded like Haeflinger's style.

He was walking fast, almost running but not quite, because there was too much slippery floor to cross, too many people pushing luggage carts to get in the way. Because nobody runs in airports unless they want some security guy to start shooting at them.

He saw her through the glass, still a good distance down the corridor, walking toward him with a woman cop on one side and a sloppy-looking guy in a suit on the other. A guy in metal-rimmed sunglasses with green lenses stepped out in front of him and said, "Just stop right there." His voice was quiet and insinuating, and Wilson caught a glimpse of the butt of an automatic sticking out from under his jacket. He got the idea, but it didn't seem very important just then. He could see Elizabeth over the guy's shoulder, on the other side of the glass. Her face looked pale and stiff, like a paper mask. She saw him then, their eyes held for a second, and then she shook her head. Wilson wondered what that meant, but he never quite figured it out.

146

BIBLIOGRAPHY

Dennis, Lane T. and Wayne Grudem, ed. *The ESV Study Bible*. Wheaton, IL: Crossway, 2008.

Frame, John M. *Systematic Theology*. Phillipsburg, New Jersey: P&R Publishing, 2013.

Latreille, Christine. "How to make a DIY obstacle course outside." *Active For Life*. May 18, 2022. https://activeforlife.com/diy-obstacle-course/.

McLeod, Kimberly. "Sidewalk Chalk Paint." *The Best Ideas for Kids*. April 12, 2020. https://www.thebestideasforkids.com/sidewalk-chalk-paint/.

Merriam-Webster Online Dictionary. "Character." *Merriam-Webster*. Accessed September 1, 2022. https://www.merriam-webster.com/dictionary/character#dictionary-entry-1.

Merriam-Webster Online Dictionary. "Hope." *Merriam-Webster*. Accessed September 1, 2022. https://www.merriam-webster.com/dictionary/hope.

Perman, Matt. "What Is the Doctrine of the Trinity?" *Desiring God*. January 23, 2006. https://www.desiringgod.org/articles/what-is-the-doctrine-of-the-trinity.

Piper, John. "Regeneration, Faith, Love: In That Order." *Desiring God*. March 2, 2008. https://www.desiringgod.org/messages/regeneration-faith-love-in-that-order.

Super Teacher Worksheets. "Word Search Puzzle Generator." *Super Teacher Worksheets*. Accessed October 27, 2022. https://www.superteacherworksheets.com/generator-word-search.html.

Ware, Bruce A. "The Father, the Son, and the Holy Spirit: The Trinity as Theological Foundation for Family Ministry." *Southern Equip*. Southern Seminary. October 10, 2011. https://equip.sbts.edu/article/the-father-the-son-and-the-holy-spirit-the-trinity-as-theological-foundation-for-family-ministry/.